Buried at the Bookshop

A Cornish Witch Mystery

Stella Berry

If you would like to be informed immediately when future books by this author are released then visit the website and sign up to the author's Reader Group www.stellaberrybooks.com

Dedicated to all the Booktokers!
Your collective wit and wisdom kept me going
even though you never knew how much it helped

Contents

Chapter One

Morgana had just finished restocking the shelves of her small shop, Merlin's Attic, when the bell on the door chimed to announce someone entering. Her shoulders slumped slightly; only two more minutes and the door would have been locked for the day.

Morgana's professional smile froze on her face as a woman barged in and flung her arms dramatically wide.

"I need your help; I have a ghost."

Morgana blinked a few times at this pronouncement and looked over her customer, trying to ascertain if she was serious.

The speaker was a largish woman in her thirties, her skin tone suggesting a mixed heritage, but what stood out most was the plethora of scarves that seemed to float around her in every direction and in every colour of the rainbow.

Morgana squinted, trying to see past the myriad of satin, velvet and silk to the aura underneath. The aura she could make out was warm, vibrant and apparently, honest.

Of course, auras were only a snapshot of what that person was feeling at that exact moment and not a good indication of their more general demeanour, but she saw nothing there to make her doubt her visitor.

"You'd better tell me all about it."

Morgana strode past her and quickly turned her shop sign to indicate she was closed. She also locked the door just in case, before turning back, she hadn't seen anything to make her feel unsafe and she'd much rather be uninterrupted if this were a genuine ghost problem.

The woman glanced around the shop, apparently seeking somewhere to sit and then settled on a bench that was part of Morgana's collection by a local wood carver.

"I'm Rhiannon Lebeau, I've rented the shop at the far end of the high street, only…" She paused as if suddenly realising she might be making a fool of herself. "Only," she continued as though forcing herself to say it, "it's haunted."

Morgana nodded and dragged out the stool she kept behind her counter. "Pleased to meet you, I think I've seen you about the village over the last couple of weeks. I'm Morgana."

Rhiannon gave a rueful smile. "I stand out a bit in Portmage, don't I?"

"In a good way," Morgana agreed, jumping forward to catch a scarf as it floated free from Rhiannon and gently wafted towards the dusty wooden floor. "Portmage could certainly benefit from a bit more diversity, and bright colours too." She held out the cheerful yellow silk to her guest. "Who told you to come to me?"

"Ellie, the lady who runs the bakery. I went in there to recover from my shock. Nothing like an exceedingly rich chocolate cake to settle the nerves, don't you think? She was so nice, I ended up telling her all about the ghost, even though I felt ridiculous even saying it. She said to come and tell you and you might be able to help."

Rhiannon cast another look around the shop, a hotchpotch of all the different things that had taken Morgana's fancy, and all had a sort of magical theme tying them together. Hence the name of her business,

Merlin's Attic.

"Ah." Morgana nodded. "Well, if Ellie sent you then you probably *do* have a ghost." She didn't mention Ellie was her sister, and therefore one of the few people who knew Morgana genuinely *could* speak to ghosts.

Rhiannon was looking Morgana up and down, taking in her black lace dress, her pointy half-boots and the large crystal hanging around her neck.

"Are you a real witch?" she asked.

The question caught Morgana off guard.

"Um, yes. Though everyone's definition of witches tends to vary."

"Oh yes, indeed," Rhiannon agreed enthusiastically. "I'm a practicing Wiccan myself, so I quite understand. I was rather hoping to find a Coven of some sort in or around Portmage, with all the King Arthur and Merlin connections and so on, but I've not found any 'sisters in magic' so far." She looked dejected at this.

"I'm afraid I'm not Wiccan, so I don't belong to any kind of Coven." Not unless she and her sisters counted as a Coven, but they'd never invited anyone to join them when they'd combined their magic. Also, as both her sisters kept their magic quiet, Morgana wouldn't feel comfortable sharing what they were capable of. "I think there might be a non-denominational Pagan group who meet in Bude. They have a Facebook page," she offered.

"So, you're a sole practitioner?" Rhiannon looked interested. "What sort of witch do you call yourself if anything?"

Morgana smiled. It was rather refreshing to be talking to someone who didn't assume all witches fell under the same type. "Technically, I'm a Hedge Witch."

Rhiannon glanced at the row of jars on a wooden bookshelf where Morgana displayed her homemade lotions and potions, and nodded.

"So those are yours? I've heard Hedge Witches are good at plant lore and healing balms, but do you actually collect things from hedgerows?"

Morgana gave Rhiannon a speculative look, and decided she was probably open-minded enough for Morgana to elaborate on the true meaning of her brand of magic.

"Most people think that's what Hedge Witch means, but actually, it doesn't. It's true I do work with plants and nature, but so do pretty much all types of witches. There are a lot of resources claiming the term Hedge Witch refers to a woman who lived *beyond the hedges* bordering a settlement or village in the old days, but the word *hedge* refers to the barrier between this world and other spiritual plains. We *cross* the hedge, or some call it *hedge jumping*. Always keeping one foot in the physical world, of course, otherwise it's dangerous."

Rhiannon leaned forward with interest. "Oh! Like astral projection?"

"For some, yes, but not me. I can see spirits and summon them if they're willing."

"Ah, hence you being the person to come to with a ghost problem?"

"Exactly," Morgana inclined her head. "So, tell me about your ghost."

"Well, she throws things at me, and she's in a really bad mood!"

Chapter Two

"She?" Morgana raised her brows in surprise. "You can see her?"

Rhiannon grimaced. "I can't see her, but I can just tell. A lingering perfume for a start, and also just the kind of things she does."

"You said she throws things? Are you absolutely sure?"

"Oh yes," Rhiannon said with a weary sigh.

"That's unusual," Morgana frowned thoughtfully. "Possibly more of a poltergeist than a ghost, perhaps? I think I'd better make some tea and you can tell me all about it, but I do need to close down the business for the day if you don't mind waiting?"

Rhiannon looked at her watch. "How about I buy you a drink in the Knights at Arms later?" she suggested. "Maybe around eight o'clock? That way, you could eat first if you wanted and not feel under pressure? Plus, I'd love to pick your brains about the local connections to Merlin and magic and so on."

Morgana bobbed her head in agreement. "That sounds perfect. I'll meet you there."

As she closed the door behind Rhiannon, waiting until all her many scarves had followed her out, Morgana glanced up at her cat. He was stretched out on the top of a bookcase, grooming his sleek black fur.

"Looks as though I might have a new friend, Lancelot. What did you think of her?"

Lancelot paused his licking at the mention of his name and gave Morgana a disinterested stare before returning to his task.

"Yes, me too," Morgana replied conversationally, even though he'd given her nothing to work with. "A bit of a big personality to fit into Portmage, but I think I liked her. Anyway, it's good to add a bit of diversity to the village, it's entirely far too generic here."

Lancelot flicked his tail.

"Do you know, Mrs. Braintree informed me the other day she's never even left Cornwall, let alone England, and she was *proud* of that."

She tutted as Lancelot continued to ignore her.

Morgana had grown up in the village and was used to how insular and prejudiced it could be, despite the steady stream of tourists from all around the world.

But she'd also spent several years away, first at university and then living and working in Bath which had all the advantages of city life, and so she took a slightly more open view of the outside world than many local people.

"I forgot to ask what kind of business she's opening, hopefully something interesting and not another shop selling nautical clothing."

She set about tidying her own store for a while and cashing up, then with Lancelot at her heels, she went upstairs to the rooms above the shop front and stockroom, where they lived.

Morgana ate a quiet dinner at her kitchen table, reading a book, then she took a quick shower before heading back downstairs and walking along the High Street to the pub.

Pushing the door open to the traditional English country pub sometimes felt as if she was stepping back in time. There was the usual local Saturday night crowd and the decor hadn't ever changed during Morgana's lifetime, as far as she could see.

The pub smelled like a warm mix of beer, pies and brine.

As well as the locals, the clientele was a mixture of smartly dressed holidaymakers and fisherman, some of whom had clearly come straight there from their boats.

People were perched on stools down the length of the long wooden bar, and the rest of the room was dotted with small tables. Wall lamps with orange shades stuck out here and there providing light, and a fire crackled in a huge hearth to one side.

Some tables had hard wooden chairs while others had squashy old armchairs, and if you were very lucky, you might even score one of the tables by the windows, with views looking towards the cliffs and the sea. These were normally snapped up by the tourists though, who didn't get to see that kind of view every day. A medieval suit of armour stood by the door, and a large Labrador lay at its feet, apparently keeping guard while also fast asleep.

Morgana stooped to give the dog a stroke, then looked around for Rhiannon.

Her new friend was already there, waving madly from a corner table.

Rhiannon rose and met Morgana halfway at the bar area, insisting on buying her a drink before they sat down.

"So, what kind of business are you opening and where exactly?" Morgana asked as soon as they were settled.

"In the building opposite the bakery. The owner said

it was an accessories store when he ran it, selling handbags, hair bands, that sort of thing." Rhiannon gave a confused frown, obviously trying to imagine a business of that nature. "But apparently, it's been a few other things in between then and now. But I'm opening a bookshop."

"A bookshop?" Morgana brightened considerably. "I'd love a proper bookshop in the village; there's a book-swap outside the Vicarage but otherwise, I have to go to Wadebridge for anything decent." She leaned a little closer, "Actually, I buy most of my books online these days, but I feel guilty doing it, especially as a small business owner myself. I'd totally be up for supporting a local shop like that."

"That's great to hear." Rhiannon was all smiles. "I'm hoping to make it really unique, a sort of mixture of new releases and popular stuff but running alongside an area for second-hand books as well. Catering to all budgets, you know? I also want to encourage people to sit and read, so I'll be doing coffee and cakes too."

Morgana nodded enthusiastically. "I like second-hand books a lot too; it's nice when they circulate and don't just sit gathering dust on someone's shelves, as they were written to be read after all."

"I've been building up a big collection of second-hand books and have been looking for just the right premises for ages. When the building in Portmage appeared for rent, I thought I'd found the perfect place, but then…" Rhiannon gave a shudder.

"So, what happened exactly? I'm actually dying to know. Oh! Sorry…no pun intended!"

"Well, I moved all my stock into the store on Friday,

yesterday," Rhiannon answered, giggling slightly at what Morgana had just said by accident.

"There's a storeroom underneath the main shop floor and the removal guys were great about carrying a ton of boxes of books down there, which they stacked up at one end of the room. It's kind of a creepy room anyway because it's underground, more of a cellar really."

Morgana nodded, she'd seen similar underground spaces in other shops along the same road.

"It's pretty cold down there but didn't feel too damp so I thought it would do nicely," Rhiannon continued. "Meanwhile, I was upstairs getting bookshelves fitted around the walls. The carpenter had drilled and screwed them all in so they were totally safe. But the guys taking things downstairs started getting a bad vibe and saying they didn't like it down in the storeroom.

"I thought they were being crazy and fortified them with mugs of tea and some of those sticky buns from the bakery. But when I went down there, I knew what they meant, it really *did* feel creepy. Honestly, they weren't making it up—and I'm not even very spook-able!"

Rhiannon paused, taking a large gulp of wine. "Nothing happened that day, but when I went back this morning, I found I didn't want to go into the storeroom alone. I told myself I was being silly, so forced myself to go down the steps, then I ran right back up again!

"The entire room had been trashed, boxes looking as though they'd been thrown in every direction. Some were split open, and books had been ripped up. It was just unbelievable! The whole place was a complete mess, all except the bit where they'd actually stacked the books, which was completely clear. Obviously, *someone* didn't want my books down there."

Morgana tapped her fingers thoughtfully against the table. "Could it have been a break-in though? A live person who had an issue with you renting the shop?"

"Oh. Um, well, probably not. Because there's more."

Rhiannon took another gulp of her wine.

"When I went back up," Rhiannon went on, "a bookcase came crashing down almost right on top of me. If I hadn't tripped over one of my scarves and stumbled to the side, it would've hit me. The same one just screwed in by a professional carpenter the day before."

"And you're sure you were alone in the room?" Morgana said, still a little bit doubtful.

Rhiannon nodded.

"I suppose it could have been crumbly plaster or something if it hadn't been for the boxes as well. And that's when I noticed one of my scarves. I might have dropped it, I suppose, though it was definitely around my neck when I entered the shop.

"But it was now on the counter, cut into tiny pieces. I mean, like I said, I'm not spookable but this scares me. Really, Morgana. That was when I decided I needed help."

Rhiannon put a hand to her throat, running her fingers along one of her many scarves. "That's when I also decided the ghost was a woman. Chopping up clothes is really petty, and it was new too!"

Morgana tried not to smile at the indignation on Rhiannon's face.

She sipped at her own wine, thinking it over.

"You could have dropped the scarf before going into the cellar, and then someone could have come into the shop while you were down below and cut it up, as well as loosening the bookcase. You don't think? Some local trying to get one up on you?"

"You don't believe it's a ghost then?" Rhiannon was clearly crestfallen at Morgana's words. "Is that what you're saying?"

"I didn't say that. I'm just looking at all the possibilities. Most hauntings I've come across have ended up having a very living human behind them, but not every time.

"There definitely are ghosts, and they can be a nuisance, but it's really rare they can toss around heavy objects like books or do something so tricky as to unscrew a bookcase. They'd have to be very angry to manage to move anything at all."

"Like maybe if they'd been murdered or something?" Rhiannon looked worried at this.

"Yes, exactly. There are ghosts in Portmage Castle that are over a thousand years old and none of them could even move so much as a pebble if they tried."

Rhiannon's mouth dropped open. "In the castle? But it's so romantic looking! I was planning to visit it this week. Maybe I won't now."

Morgana laughed. "Really, you should go! They can't hurt you, and you won't know they're there unless you're particularly open to feeling them. They assault me like a battering ram though, given my psychic ability. They all like to try and scare me. But it's a wonderful castle and it'd be a real shame to miss out because of a few spooks."

"Hmm, I think I'll still give it a miss for the moment. I mean, I can't even go back into my own shop now because I might get attacked by the furniture."

Morgana reached out and put a hand over Rhiannon's, realising the other woman was more shaken up than she'd first appeared. "Look, don't worry. I'll go with you and we'll find out exactly what sort of ghost we're dealing with, okay?" She looked at her watch and saw it was already half past nine. "But not tonight. I have a long day tomorrow."

"There's no way I'm going back in there at night-time," Rhiannon said, fervently. "It's scary enough during the middle of the day."

"Okay, well my day off is Monday, so how about we meet there on Monday morning, around eleven?"

Rhiannon agreed to this with obvious relief, and they passed another agreeable half an hour together where Morgana filled in her new friend on some of the local history of Portmage, regaling her with stories about some of its more interesting inhabitants.

It wasn't until Morgana got home, feeling rather cheerful after two glasses of wine, that she began to really think about how unlikely it was for a ghost to do all the things Rhiannon had described. It seemed far more likely Rhiannon had unwittingly made an enemy in the village, and someone was creating dangerous trouble.

In which case, her new friend was definitely going to need help, but maybe help from the police rather than from her? Either that or it might very well be a poltergeist rather than a ghost, and that was a whole other bag of bad trouble.

Morgana would need both her sisters with her to get

rid of a poltergeist.

Even then, it wouldn't be easy!

Chapter Three

Even though it was a Sunday, Morgana still opened her shop the next morning as usual.

Weekend tourists were good trade and being self-employed in a touristy village meant she couldn't afford to take Sundays off.

She started her usual morning routine of cleansing the shop of any residual energies from the day before, by walking three times anti-clockwise around the shop floor while holding a sage smudge stick. Then once the smoke had settled, she picked up her besom.

Now, she began to sweep, again using small anti-clockwise circles to collect up the energy and then sweeping it right out the front door as she changed the sign over from Closed to Open. She stood for a few moments and held each of the protective charms hanging around the door, using her own energy to charge them up for the day.

Then she walked into the stockroom out the back where she kept an electric kettle and switched it on for some coffee. Cup in hand, she settled down behind the shop counter and pulled out the crossword she hadn't managed to finish the previous day.

The crossword was both her prop and her addiction.

It made customers feel less pressured if she were focussed on something other than them when they entered; Morgana knew from her own experiences there was nothing more uncomfortable than a shopkeeper's eyes following you around the displays.

She preferred to cast a cheery greeting when they came in, and then just be on hand if they needed her, and that approach worked really well for sales and footfall.

Plus, the crosswords were also a case of engaging in battle against the sharp minds of their creators, thinking of each creator as her personal nemesis. When she'd lived in Bath, she'd been a fan of the crossword in the Times, but since moving back to Cornwall, she'd switched to a more local paper and discovered to both her chagrin and delight that the crossword in the Cornish County News was even more tricky than the one in the Times.

"Enchanting and thaumaturgic, seven letters," Morgana muttered to herself. "Hmm. I feel like this should be easy for me." She twirled her pen in her fingers. "Enchanting, charming? Bewitching? No, both too long. Thaumaturgy; that's when you perform miracles, right?"

She looked down at her pen which spun in her palm before coming to a stop. "Oh, duh. Magical!" She filled in the squares with huge satisfaction.

"A male of local metal. Three and three."

She chewed her lip considering the next clue.

"Something to do with chainmail, maybe? Or a suit of armour?"

She thought back to the knight standing guard inside the door of the Knights at Arms pub.

The bell over her own door chimed as it opened, a couple in their mid-sixties stepping in out of the cold. Morgana tilted her head curiously. Their age group tended not to frequent shops like hers very often, preferring the more upmarket boutiques and art galleries.

The man shook out his smart coat, looking a bit

uncomfortable, but the woman made a beeline for the counter.

"Oh, hello. Can you help me? I'm looking for something handmade and unique as a wedding present. It's our daughter, you see; she's owned her own home for years, and quite honestly, we despaired of her finding a man, so she already has everything she could possibly need, and now—at nearly forty, would you believe—she's getting married!

"Well, we couldn't be more thrilled but it does make it terribly difficult to buy them a traditional present because they've got everything you could think of, so, she's asked everyone to get them something unusual to make their home more interesting and we saw your lovely window and thought you might have just the thing?" The woman spoke very fast and Morgana had begun to wonder if she would ever draw breath.

"Oh, I'm sure we can find the perfect something together," she said, as reassuringly as she was able. "It rather depends on how much you want to spend? I have some lovely salad bowls and tongs made by a local man. Each one is unique and there's oak, pine, beech and even some made from driftwood?"

She gestured to a display corner where she had a whole range of items made by Old Tom, as he was affectionately known in the village.

The woman looked interested, but the husband shook his head.

"Only daughter, you know. Got to be special."

"Well, they are special because every piece is different—there are never two the same in material or look," Morgana said, trying not to sound defensive. "But

I think I understand. You want something also personal and a bit more of a *statement?*"

"Oh yes, precisely that." The woman looked embarrassed at turning down the bowls.

Morgana smiled sympathetically.

"Don't worry, I think I have the ideal gift."

She turned their attention to the wooden bench Rhiannon had sat herself on the night before. "Do they have a garden? See this carving here," she ran her fingers along the backrest, "this is a Celtic love knot, perfect for newlyweds. And, if you're not in a massive hurry, then I could get the woodworker to carve their initials either side of the love knot.

"It would be something they'd keep forever and could sit outside in the sunshine side by side for years to come. They'd always remember their wedding day—and you too, of course, as you were the ones who gave it to them. So, they'd have special thoughts of you too!"

She knew she was laying it on a bit thick with the heavy sell, but the bench *was* rather expensive. She watched as the husband checked the price label hanging off the bench.

"Oh, Gerald, this is perfect!" The wife stroked the smooth seat.

"Can it be delivered to Cirencester by mid-January?" he asked.

Apparently, neither of them was put off by the price.

"Absolutely." Morgana sighed with relief at the good window of time he was suggesting. "Delivery would be extra though, especially considering the size and weight. And did you want their names or initials carved onto it? That would increase the price too."

He gave a sharp jerk of his chin in agreement.

"Initials please, R for Rebecca and M for Michael."

She quickly calculated the final figure and held it out to him.

She had to guesstimate what a courier would be based on a rough mileage to Cirencester, but she'd drive the thing there herself if need be.

"Good." His head was nodding, always a positive sign.

The man gave another brisk nod and handed Morgana a credit card.

"I'm rather relieved to have this done and dusted. No more trailing around markets searching for the non-existent. Which means we can get back to our touring now, can't we Dulcie?" He sounded almost pleading as he turned to his wife, and Morgana could well imagine he'd been dragged to a lot of different places before finding hers.

"Yes, Gerald, we can." His wife's eyes twinkled up at him as she squeezed his arm affectionately. "He's terribly keen to visit all the local tin mines around Cornwall. Goodness knows why. When you've seen one, you've seen them all, but the scenery *is* quite spectacular, though I'm glad we have the new car as it's awfully chilly out on the moors. Heated seats," she whispered the last bit to Morgana as though imparting a naughty secret.

"Just what you need in Cornwall in winter," Morgana agreed, handing over the receipt. "Oh," she exclaimed as a realisation hit her. "A male of local metal, tin! Tin Man. Sorry, it was a crossword clue," she explained as the couple looked at her with confusion.

They all laughed.

She took a few more details, then cheerfully waved them off before hurrying back to her paper and filling in the solution. She was feeling quite buoyed by the sale of the bench too.

It was actually Old Tom who'd get most of the profit, and she only made a commission on selling one of his pieces, but the several hundred pounds he'd earn from it would keep him going for months and she was really glad to have been able to help by displaying his work.

That was something she'd missed horribly when she'd lived in a city, the way everyone pulled together in a village and looked out for each other. Of course, on the other hand, there was always the downside of everyone knowing your personal business too.

Morgana ate lunch seated at the counter, feeling unwilling to close up and put off customers to take a lunch hour. She hired help during the summer season, but it was winter now, and trade too slow to justify a full-time second member of staff.

Many businesses even shut completely during the winter months, especially those only selling to tourists. But Morgana was lucky enough that even the locals patronised her premises, buying face creams and ointments, and picking up birthday gifts for friends.

She smoothed out the crossword again as she unwrapped a sandwich she'd prepared and pondered over some more clues. "Meeting that's likely to be awkward, five and four," she muttered. She already had a few of the letters now, and it didn't tax her too much. "First Date." She wrote, decisively. "That's a coincidence," she said, addressing Lancelot who was sleeping on the pile of gift wrap paper. "Tonight, is my first date with Lord Latheborne."

She propped her head on her hand, eyes glazing slightly as she thought about Oliver.

His full title was Oliver Westley, Baron of Latheborne.

They'd met a month earlier, when she'd been staying at his manor as a guest of someone else. Oliver hadn't seemed to like her at all initially, but there had been an instant, if unwanted, attraction between them. Of course, he'd thought she was her twin sister at the time and had only asked her on a date once the truth of her real identity had come out.

She didn't know a huge amount about him yet, only that he owned a crumbling mansion, had a hilarious grandmother, and he valued honesty above all. He was also handsome, educated, and his cold demeanour hid an excellent sense of humour. One of the other guests at the time had described him as "quite the dashing Darcy" and Morgana felt it fit him well.

"Yup, first dates are always a bit awkward, but here's hoping."

She looked at her watch, intending to close fairly soon as she always shut up early on a Sunday. It was an unusual night for a first date, but as Monday was her normal day off and Oliver also worked for himself in managing his estate, it had made sense to arrange it for then.

A few more customers came and went as a crisp sunshine encouraged them out for walks through the village, or they dropped by in passing on their way to and from Portmage Castle, the village's main tourist attraction. At 3 p.m., she saw the last person out and shut the door with a final click, turning the lock.

"Now comes the lengthy task of deciding what to wear," Morgana told Lancelot as they ascended the stairs to her apartment.

She took a long bath, fed the cat, and then moved into her bedroom.

"I need to look a bit classy as he's rather posh, but I also need to look like myself as he needs to get to know the *real* me. I can't go full on *witch* as he doesn't know about that yet, but I also don't want to hide it because it's better I tell him sooner rather than later. He wouldn't appreciate it if I hid it from him, but he may very well run a mile when he does find out!"

Morgana littered her bed with outfits as she spoke. Lancelot's head tilted side to side, ears perked. But he had nothing to say on the matter. He always looked interested, however, which was more than enough for Morgana. "So, you agree, then, boy? That's good."

After finally choosing a simple grey wool dress with a cobweb pattern stitched across one shoulder, she spent some time pawing through her jewellery box, eventually settling on the necklace she wore almost every day. It was a large amethyst crystal bound in a cage of silver, and she chose this because she was nervous and it would ground her.

She then dithered for a while between elegant drop earrings and amethyst stars that matched the necklace. After wandering around for a while wearing one of each, she decided on the stars; they were simply more *her*.

Last time Oliver had seen her, she'd been wearing clothes and make-up designed to make her look more like her twin. However, while they were identical to look at, they had fairly different styles, and Morgana sincerely hoped Oliver would like the earthier style she favoured. When she acted as Morwenna, her style, on the other hand, tended more toward bright yet sultry.

At ten to seven, she patted Lancelot goodbye, pulled on a warm coat, and set off.

Walking the five hundred or so meters up the High Street to the Round Table, the restaurant where they were having their date, every step set her nerves jangling, even more than her charm bracelet did. She stopped at the window, seeing Oliver seated inside.

She took a swift moment to refamiliarise herself with his features.

He sat very straight, probably due to his naval background.

His hair was dark brown and he probably thought it needed a cut but she liked the way it always looked rather windswept. It was the only scruffy thing about him. His clothes were neat, an open collared shirt under a V-neck chunky sweater. She couldn't see his eyes from where she was standing but knew they were a deep blue like the ocean, and that his aura would match them. As she watched, he twirled the stem of his wine glass, and she smiled to herself, realising he was probably just as nervous as she was.

She hadn't been on a formal date like this in a long time, but Oliver was a formal sort of man. She wasn't at all sure the 'real' her was the kind of woman he'd go for usually and vowed to give him an easy out if he wanted it.

She entered the restaurant, taking off her coat,

impressed as a waiter glided smoothly forward to take it from her. She pointed to Oliver and the waiter nodded, gesturing she should go and join him.

"Hi." She gave him a shy smile as she approached the table. Oliver jumped to his feet, pulling out the chair opposite for her to sit down.

Morgana raised her eyebrows at the old-fashioned chivalry but decided not to comment.

"Good evening, Morgana. I'm so glad you could make it. You look lovely."

He made no attempt to greet her with a kiss or any physical contact, and she was glad because she knew touching him would cause her to feel a desire that might prove futile once she'd told him what she was.

The waiter glided over once she was seated, proffering two menus.

"Um, can we just get a drink to start and maybe order some food in a bit?" she asked Oliver, hesitantly.

It wasn't like her to feel so unsure, but she already knew she could come to really like Oliver and that made her wary about having any expectations from him.

Honesty first, then food, if he was still willing.

He tilted his head, almost questioningly, but only said, "Of course. What would you like?"

She was about to suggest they got a bottle of something when she remembered he was probably driving. His home was about forty minutes away, right in the middle of the bleakest part of Dartmoor. It seemed unfair she'd only have to walk a short way down the road, but then again there was nothing for miles where he lived and he had been the one to ask if she knew of a good place to eat local to her.

She already knew Oliver wasn't expecting to stay the night with her as he simply wasn't that kind of man. He'd keep it utterly respectful until they naturally reached that stage in their relationship. If they ever got past tonight, that was…

"Just a glass of white wine, and a glass of sparkling water too please," Morgana said to the waiter.

"A glass of red for me, and a bottle of still water please," Oliver concurred.

"How is the Baroness?" Morgana asked, as the waiter left to get their drinks.

The Baroness was Oliver's grandmother who lived with him, she was officially *the Dowager Baroness* by title, but she said the Dowager bit made her feel old and so she'd prefer not to adopt it at least until her grandson took a wife.

Morgana's mouth tilted up, thinking of the elderly lady, who at first glance seemed rather barmy. But Morgana didn't think she was barmy at all, just refreshingly blunt.

The Baroness said whatever she felt like saying and didn't care who heard her.

"She's doing remarkably well," Oliver said, a wry smile touching his own lips, "especially considering how much sherry she drinks. I think she's pickling herself so she lives forever. She'll probably outlive both of us at this rate."

"Good, she's wonderful comedy value, and I'm sure she's great fun to have around," Morgana said thinking back on some of the more outrageous things the Baroness had said.

"Hmm, more like demanding than fun, and always

telling me my faults."

Oliver took the two wine glasses from the waiter and set the white down in front of Morgana. He waited until the water had been poured and the waiter had discretely vanished again before adding, "She remembers you, you know? You somehow made a big hit, and she asked when you were coming to stay again."

Morgana flushed slightly, partly from pleasure at being remembered by a woman who ignored most things, but also because going to stay at Latheborne Manor again would mean things were progressing between her and Oliver.

Morgana took a sip of wine then put it down, making eye contact with Oliver.

"There's something I wanted to tell you."

"Yes, I had a feeling." He took a sip of his own wine and held her gaze. "Just say it, Morgana, I don't want any secrets, and something is clearly making you uncomfortable."

She took a deep breath and tried to calm herself. "Do you remember the weekend at Latheborne Manor when I was sort of helping the police?"

"The weekend when you were pretending to be your twin sister? I could hardly forget it, what with two murders in my house." His eyes twinkled at her, hints of laughter in their depths. "I remember you were on first-name terms with the various officers attending the crime scene and you were the one who actually uncovered the murderer. You have my profound thanks for that."

Morgana pressed her lips together, picking up on both the admonishment and the teasing. "I was on first name terms with them because helping them is something I've done more than once. Several times, in fact."

"Really?" Oliver's face lit with interest.

"I'm, um, sort of psychic."

"You mean you're good at reading people? I got the impression you were."

"Yes, but it's more than that. The police use me sometimes on murder cases because I can see things they can't, no matter how perceptive they are."

He regarded her thoughtfully. "You think you can read minds?"

She huffed out a sigh, knowing it was going to be difficult to explain. He wasn't the type to accept such things on face value.

"No, I don't read minds." She paused. "I see auras, to be precise."

Oliver gave her a long look as though searching her eyes for how truthful she was being. Then he leaned back in his chair and took another sip of his wine.

"Auras. Okay," he said sceptically. "And how does that help?"

"It means I can see when someone is lying, and all sorts of other emotions too, like hate or jealousy or lust, that kind of thing. It helps the police to get an understanding of what suspects are hiding."

"And they truly believe you can do this?" He still sounded doubtful, but not convinced she was crazy, which was something. After all, if the police used her services, that gave her statements a certain degree of credibility.

"Yes. Both the Detective Sergeant and the Constable grew up in Portmage and they know my family has certain… powers."

His brows lifted. "Powers?"

"Magic powers," she said it defensively. This was the moment when he'd probably walk out the door, but he didn't. Instead, he took another contemplative sip of wine.

"I don't think I believe in magic, Morgana."

"Well, I do, and whether you believe me or not does not affect the fact it's true—and is what it is. So, that's why I was hesitant to dine yet. Because I thought you would brush me off as a crazy woman. If you wanted to call it a night and not see me again, then I understand. I cannot simply alter my powers and get them to go away when I meet someone who doubts them."

He didn't leave though.

Instead, he reached out and twined his fingers through hers where they rested on the table.

"I like you. I'm not exactly sure why or what it is about you, but I want to get to know you better, to know all about you. If you believing in magic is a part of who you are, then I want to know that bit too. So, how about we have our dinner, and if you still like me back by the end of it, then we'll make arrangements for another date, and maybe another after that?"

Morgana's fingers seemed to tingle where they made contact with his, and she felt her heart rate speed up at the simple but intimate touch of his hand.

"Are you sure? I'm not trying to scare you off or anything, but a lot of people think I'm pretty odd."

"Odd is okay. You've met my grandmother, she's not exactly run of the mill either."

Morgana chuckled. "That she isn't. You know she

can see the ghosts in your house?"

"They aren't real, she's just being quirky."

"Oh, they're real," Morgana assured him. "You've got at least two that I've seen."

Oliver withdrew his hand, small frown lines appearing between his brows. "Are you sure you aren't trying to put me off? Look, I don't believe in ghosts either."

She shrugged her shoulders.

"And of course, they will go away if you do not believe in them!" she said.

She was challenging him and enjoying it, though she was not being deliberately adversarial. She smiled. "I mean, does the earth turn flat because the Flat Earthers say it's so? Oliver, I'm just laying it all on the line up front. I know you were angry with me about deceiving you when we first met, so I'm not going to hide anything at all and won't be at all offended if you decide it's too kooky for you."

She realised as she said it that she'd just told her first lie. She *would* be offended, but she'd never show it and he deserved to make an informed choice.

Oliver took a deep breath.

"Look, I'm hungry, so how about we order? Then I'll share some of my stranger quirks and enjoy each other's company, okay?"

At her smile, he signalled the waiter and they perused the menu.

They ordered and talked for a while about Morgana's shop and the improvements Oliver was making to his family estate.

There was a pause as their starters were cleared, then

Oliver cleared his throat.

Morgana looked at him inquisitively, knowing he had something he wanted to ask.

"The, um, ghosts at the manor—what exactly is it you think you saw?" he said.

"Are you testing me?" she teased. "Or do you believe just a teeny tiny bit?"

"Obviously, there's no such thing as ghosts, but… Well, when I was a boy, I used to be convinced I could see things my parents couldn't, and then…"

"You forgot all about them," Morgana finished for him. "That's normal. Children are more open so they see more than adults, then you hit your teens and deride everything you thought was true as a child, and it goes away. Ghosts, fairies, the bogeyman under the bed."

He coughed on his water. "Please tell me you're not going to say that's real too?"

"Most of it is real, but extremely uncommon. Or, more likely, isn't anything supernatural at all, just a draft or someone playing tricks."

"Well, that's a relief, sort of," he said, dryly.

"But your ghosts are real. There's a maid who sweeps the fire in your formal dining room. She comes in about once an hour and the fire always dies slightly when she gets close. I'd say she was Victorian by her outfit. On the other hand, you have a ghost in the kitchens who's much, much older. She only speaks in the old Cornish dialect, so I couldn't understand a word. That language died out at least 100 years ago, so she's probably been there far longer."

He didn't react for a long moment and looked as though he was thinking.

Morgana considered it a good sign. She didn't need him to believe, but it would certainly help their cause if he didn't dismiss everything she said out of hand. Plus, if she were to become more involved with him romantically, then she'd like to be able to share with him some of her world and the things she became involved in.

"Of course, while ghosts are common in really old properties like yours," she continued conversationally, "they're also not that hard to get rid of. I've got a ghost problem to deal with tomorrow actually, though I suspect it's not a ghost at all, but a poltergeist."

A glimmer of interest flickered through his eyes. "Is there a difference? Poltergeists are supposed to move things, right?"

"Right." She gave him a bright smile. "The difference is they aren't the spirits of dead people."

"They're not? What are they then, some kind of demon or something?"

"Oh, goodness no, thankfully! Poltergeists are actually just energy, caused by living humans. They usually occur in a household where something very emotional has happened, and it leaves a sort of ball of negative energy behind that lashes out sometimes. It can be something as every day as divorce and arguments, or domestic abuse, but quite often it's created by teenage girls."

"Teenage girls?" He laughed in disbelief.

"Yes, their emotions can run extremely high, all those hormones. They can love and hate with a passion not seen at any other time in life. When you have a house with several teenage girls living there at the same time, it's not uncommon for cups to hurl themselves off shelves and smash, or windows to rattle, fires to randomly ignite, that kind of thing. It's all the emotional energy flying around that causes it."

Oliver gave a chuckle. "This one I think I *do* believe in. It makes an odd sort of sense."

"That's a start." Morgana's eyes twinkled back at him.

"And what will you do to help if this job tomorrow does turn out to be a poltergeist?"

"I'll try to cleanse the place, hopefully that will work."

"Well, I'll say this for you, Morgana. You're not boring."

They stuck to safe and non-supernatural conversation after that, and apart from a squabble over the bill when Morgana insisted on paying half, and Oliver refusing, and them eventually agreeing she would pay next time and they'd always take it in turns, the evening ended very well.

Oliver insisted on walking Morgana home.

Another awkward first date moment occurred on her doorstep.

She turned when she reached the door, ready to thank him, but Oliver's expression was a picture—and not necessarily in a good way. His face bore an indecisive look before he quickly cleared it away. She knew exactly what he was thinking, not through any kind of use of her powers but because she was thinking it too.

Is he going to kiss me?

Should *she* just kiss him?

Why should *he* be the one to instigate it?

The attraction they'd felt from the start was still there between them, but she had dropped some pretty big bombshells on him about the kind of person she was.

Maybe he needed some time to process that?

Seconds ticked by and then Oliver reached a decision.

He moved forward, kissing her on the cheek.

Morgana's jaw tightened slightly with disappointment, her fingers flexing as she longed to pull him forward and see what a real kiss would be like between them.

Oliver's eyes narrowed a fraction and he stepped back.

"Sorry." His tone was flat and she found him suddenly unreadable.

"Sorry?" She was confused.

"You tensed up, I guess it was too soon?"

Her eyes widened, impressed at how he didn't try to hide his doubts.

Pride normally stopped people from being that open with their thoughts. But that was one of the things that had drawn her to Oliver from their first meeting; he didn't hide. He had walls but didn't use them to conceal his feelings, just to protect himself from others.

She barely refrained from rolling her eyes at how wrong he'd got it though.

Instead, she shook her head, and her mouth twitched up at the corners.

"I was actually hoping our first kiss would be a bit more memorable. Want to try that again?"

He gave her a suspicious look then leaned forward as

though to kiss her cheek again. She very deliberately turned her head, giving him time to change his mind, and their lips met.

She wasn't disappointed. He kissed the way he did everything.

Controlled, strong and commanding, but with a restraint only hinting at the fire beneath his always calm demeanour.

She wanted to coax the fire out from behind his walls, but this wasn't the time, not yet.

She sighed with satisfaction against his lips as he gently broke the kiss.

"Better?" he asked, his voice laced with humour.

"Much," she agreed with a grin. "Goodnight, Oliver." She went through her door and shut it behind her, discovering she was still grinning and couldn't seem to stop.

"Meow." Lancelot wound around her ankles, pleased she was home.

"Yes, thank you, it was a very nice night," she replied, bending to run her hand down the cat's back.

Lancelot made a chirruping sound, pleased with the attention.

Morgana tickled him under the chin. "He didn't run a mile at any rate!"

Chapter Four

Out of habit, Morgana woke fairly early on Monday, despite the lateness of the previous evening's date. She was about to roll over to catch another hour of sleep when she remembered she was meeting Rhiannon at eleven.

She felt surprisingly eager to discover the truth of her ghost.

Some were awful to be around, like those at Portmage Castle, but others were pretty interesting to have contact with. They had absolutely no concept of time, which could make communication difficult, but helping them to find some peace and cross over was definitely rewarding; she could always use an extra bit of good karma.

Morgana chatted to Lancelot as she put out his breakfast and made herself coffee.

"It might be a fairly straightforward haunting, of course, though I've never heard anything about the premises having a ghost before. I don't really remember any of the previous businesses to open there." She blew thoughtfully on her hot coffee. "Ellie would though, especially as it's right opposite her bakery. I should definitely pop in and see her before I meet Rhiannon, and see if she can give me any background info on the place."

Lancelot looked up briefly from his cat food dish.

"Yes, yes, I'll get some scones with clotted cream and jam while I'm there, and you can steal my cream." She grinned, rubbing the top of his head.

So, a little after ten, Morgana walked up the High

Street, away from the centre of Portmage and towards the castle, to where Ellie ran her bakery and tea rooms.

She considered the hour fairly early as she didn't get a lot of customers herself at this time, but the tea room part of Ellie's business was already full of customers who'd had enough of the crisp sea air and needed a warm cup of tea and something sweet to go with it.

The bakery too had a short queue inside, and the smell of fresh baking wafted out the door, enticing yet more people to go in.

"The early bird gets the cream," Morgana commented to herself.

"Good morning, Morgana," a strong cheery voice called out from behind her.

Morgana turned and saw Mrs. Goodbody making her way towards her from the direction of the cliffs and castle. Dragging behind her was a small white West Highland Terrier, who looked decidedly miserable in the cold, despite his natty tartan coat.

"Morning, Mrs. Goodbody. Hello, Horace."

"It's worm, dear," Mrs. Goodbody said in a schoolteacher voice.

Morgana stared at her. "Worm? I ... What?"

She was totally confused, especially as she *knew* the dog was called Horace.

"Don't gape that way, Morgana, it makes you look like a salmon. *The early bird gets the worm*, not the cream."

"Oh, haha, right. I knew that. It was just an in-joke between me and, well, my cat."

Mrs. Goodbody tutted at her. "Cat people, always a bit odd, it's because you don't get out enough. A cat will sit on your lap and encourage laziness. A dog, however, needs walking. It gets you up and out for some healthy exercise!"

She delivered this statement with vigour as though it were a well-known fact.

Morgana glanced down again at Horace, noting the fact the dog, far from looking like he needed walking, had taken advantage of the conversation his mistress was having and was lying on his side having a power nap right there on the road.

Mrs. Goodbody swept her eyes over Morgana's outfit as she so often did, but clearly couldn't find much to comment on. "Those heels are awfully high," she said, finally settling on Morgana's black boots. "Terribly bad for your back."

"They are, aren't they?" Morgana agreed through a gritted smile. "But I have to wear such boring shoes to stand on my feet all day that I indulge my taste on my days off."

"Well, they make you too tall. Men don't like to have to look up at a woman, dear." Mrs. Goodbody gave a tug on the leash and moved on, leaving Morgana wishing she were rude enough to retort in kind. She wore the boots for herself, not for any man.

After a few deep breaths of calming sea air, Morgana pushed open the door to her sister's business, Pixie's Place, Bakery & Tea Room. Entering the tea shop and cafe side of the business, she snagged an empty table and smiled at the instantly approaching waitress.

"Hi Morgana, the usual?"

"Yes please, Lucy, and could you ask Ellie if she can spare me a few minutes to chat?"

It didn't take Lucy long to return with a pot of

coffee and some poached eggs on toast, which Morgana ordered almost every Monday to kick-start her day off.

"Ellie said she's just icing some cakes and doesn't want the sugar to harden, but she'll be out before you're finished."

"Great, thank you." Morgana tucked into the breakfast, and true to her word, Ellie appeared before she was done.

"Hi Mog, how's the food?" Ellie took the chair on the other side of the table.

"Same as always, eggs done to perfection. I have no idea why making a perfect poached egg at home is so tricky."

Ellie smiled smugly. "So, how was your date last night? I hear he didn't spend the night, but you both had three courses and lingered over drinks for ages."

"You should work for MI6, Ellie. How do you always know everything?"

"In this case, it was easy, Lucy's sister is a waitress at the Round Table, and she was in here about an hour ago." Ellie laughed at the expression on Morgana's face. "I've told you before, you'll continue to be the source of gossip until you finally get married and become too boring to mention."

"Humph. And who was watching to check if he stayed the night?" Morgana asked, her eyes narrowed suspiciously.

"No one, it was just that he parked right outside the restaurant, and his car drove away not long after you left. Unless, of course, he was just moving it to the parking area behind your shop?" Ellie's eyes lit with interest, then dimmed again when Morgana shook her head.

"So, who was he? No one from the village apparently, and not Tristan either or Gemma would have recognised him."

"Why would I be out with Tristan?" Morgana felt herself blush even as she cursed herself for asking the question; she should have just ignored Ellie's digging.

"Oh, come on! We all know sparks fly when the two of you get near each other."

"They don't," she denied too vehemently. "And he was Morwenna's boyfriend, not mine." It was the reason she could never allow herself to have feelings for Tristan.

The fact he'd once been romantically involved with her twin was just too uncomfortable.

"That was more than ten years ago when you were all teenagers; nobody cares about it now but you." Ellie threw up her hands in exasperation.

Morgana gave her a stubborn look and Ellie sighed, letting it go.

"At least tell me who you were with last night. Apparently, he paid with a card saying he was a baron or something?"

"His name is Oliver, and yes, he is a baron. Though not one of those high-flying society types. He owns Latheborne Manor on Dartmoor where I went to stay last month, remember?"

"So, he's rich? That's a good start." Ellie grinned. "And I hear he's quite charming and extremely good looking too?"

"Not so rich, I suspect his estate is a money pit."

Morgana smiled as Ellie's face fell a little.

"Oh well, you were never that impressed by money anyway."

"He's not so much with the charming either, except when he wants to be."

"Oh." Ellie's face fell even further.

"But he's honest, and genuine, and straightforward. And yes, I'd definitely describe him as handsome."

Ellie brightened again considerably. "High praise from someone as picky as you. Will you be going out again?"

"I hope so." Morgana paused, putting her knife and fork together on her plate. "I thought it went quite well, but I did tell him I was a witch, and I know he didn't believe me, but he seemed okay with it at the time. However..." She paused again and swallowed down some coffee. "He might well have changed his mind in the cold light of day. He's a very down-to-earth sort of person, and I think I've probably scared him off."

Morgana had woken up that morning, completely riddled with insecurities about having been so open the previous night, and slightly regretting her determination to tell Oliver everything upfront.

Ellie saw the self-doubt in Morgana's eyes and reached over to pat her hand. "If he can't love you for who you really are, then what's the point anyway?"

"True," Morgana agreed. "But I could really like him, and maybe I should have revealed things a bit more slowly. Let him get used to it in stages, you know?"

"Oh, Morgana. It will work out if it's meant to, you know. Gregory doesn't like me being witchy and gets a bit testy if I talk about it, but he loves me and it's all that matters. Is that what you wanted to talk to me about?"

"Actually, no. Nothing to do with Oliver at all, I wanted to ask what you know about the business across the road?"

They both looked out the window, and Morgana pointed out the premises.

Not the one directly opposite, but one building down, where even now, a sign was being painted over the door reading *Lebeau Books*.

Ellie clapped her hands together. "Oh, of course, the lady with the ghosts. I wondered if she'd come to see you. Have you been in there yet?"

"I'm meeting her there at eleven to check it out. But I thought I'd get some of the history of the place first, and as you know absolutely everything about everyone…"

Morgana left her words hanging, teasing her sister for being a gossip.

Ellie rolled her eyes. "It's not my fault, you know. People come in here and sit and talk about stuff and I can't help overhearing a lot of it. Obviously, I've heard a few things about the place as it's right there." Ellie pointed at the bookshop. "But mostly, it's been empty.

"Let me think. First, it was a sort of clothes store, but not clothes; they sold handbags and hats and stuff like that. They'd been there ever since we were little, then the lady who ran the place went missing and it was closed for a couple of years at least.

"Afterwards, someone opened it again as a dry cleaner's, but whether it was the ghost or just a total lack of business, I don't know, but they closed again pretty quickly.

"After that, it was a hair and nail bar. They didn't last long either, but Yvonne who was employed there definitely said it was haunted; she only did three days and then refused to go back. I seem to remember the ghost threw hair dye all over the chairs and then used nail varnish to paint obscenities on the wall."

Morgana widened her eyes. "Seriously? A ghost with the power to write in nail varnish? They'd have to remove the lid and the focus required to write legibly would be immense. I've never met one that strong."

"Me neither, but I believe it's possible." Ellie tipped her head thoughtfully. "On the other hand, the tale smacks of a disgruntled employee using the ghost story to cover their own bad behaviour."

Morgana nodded. "That sounds much more likely to me too. So, you've never been inside the place to check?"

"Why would I? I can't *see* ghosts. You're the only one of us with that power. Anyway, it was an estate agency after that, or at least was supposed to be. They changed their minds even though they'd taken out a twelve-month lease. Again, I don't know if that was due to a ghost problem because the company was part of a chain rather than someone local.

"But I do know people around here would think twice before taking on the place, though probably more to do with the disappearance of the woman than anything else. Don't you remember the scandal?"

"Not at all. What happened and when?"

Ellie squinted, trying to remember.

"It must be about ten years ago now, so was probably when you'd just left to go to university. It was owned by a married couple and the wife had been working late on her own, then never came home. Her husband reported her missing, but the police suspected him of doing her in, I think. There were rumours he'd been having affairs if I remember rightly. But I don't think there was any evidence of murder, so eventually, it was dropped."

"So, she could be the ghost? If there really is a ghost, of course. Do you remember her name?" Morgana couldn't help thinking it rather sounded like another local legend given life just through word of mouth.

"Um, Valerie? No, Valeria. Valeria Dawson. Her husband, Archie Dawson, still lives in the village, on the outskirts just past Crooked Style."

"He does?"

Morgana was surprised as she knew most people in the village, at least to nod to.

"He keeps to himself since his wife disappeared. I'm amazed he hasn't moved away, to be honest. It must have been dreadful to have everyone whispering behind his back saying he murdered his wife." Ellie was particularly sensitive to this as her own husband had once been accused of murder and she hated to think anyone might be maligned unjustly.

"Yes," Morgana agreed. "Unless, of course, he did murder her and she's our ghost."

"Maybe." Ellie shrugged. "Or maybe there's been a ghost in the building for centuries but people were too scared to say so."

"Or a poltergeist?" Morgana suggested.

Ellie gave a shiver. "I hope not. Shouldn't you be heading over there to find out? It's almost eleven."

"Already?" Morgana glanced at her watch and rose to her feet.

"Breakfast's on the house today," Ellie said, waving

Morgana's hand away as she tried to take out her card to pay. "If I can't occasionally treat my little sister, then what's the point of owning your own business?"

Morgana smiled and thanked her.

"Never mind that, just make sure you keep me informed about what you find. I'd love to hear there's a genuine ghost in there. It'd be such a talking point!"

Chapter Five

Morgana found Rhiannon outside the bookshop, peering in the windows.

"Oh hi." She looked slightly embarrassed as she turned and saw Morgana approaching. "I feel so silly not wanting to go inside on my own, but…" She trailed off, shrugging helplessly.

"I don't blame you at all if there's a ghost in there, especially if it's tried to hurt you. Would you rather I go in by myself to check?" Morgana reached out and plucked up one of Rhiannon's scarves as the breeze pulled it off her shoulder and tried to carry it down the street.

"No, it's okay. I'm just glad you're here and don't think I'm totally crazy." Rhiannon took a key out of her handbag and unlocked the front door of the storefront. It was dim inside, but Rhiannon went quickly over to a bank of light switches and began to flick them all on.

Morgana looked around.

The bookcase her new friend had mentioned was still face down on the floor; it looked heavy and Morgana could quite see why it would have been terrifying to have it nearly fall on you. On the shop counter were the tattered remains of a scarf cut into tiny pieces, and the floor was littered with torn books. She raised her brows at the carnage.

"This is definitely the work of someone who doesn't want you here, but I don't see a ghost." Her eyes swept all the set-back alcoves before she raised her voice. "Hello? I'm Morgana Emrys and I'm speaking to anyone who might be here. I ask you to show yourself to me."

She paused for a moment and then turned back to Rhiannon.

"In general, ghosts have the ability to remain unseen if they want to. I can only see them if they *choose* to let me. I have the power to force the issue, but that mostly just makes them annoyed."

"She might be in the storeroom? It's underneath us," Rhiannon suggested, looking nervous but determined.

"Okay, let's check it out."

Rhiannon pointed a finger to a door at the back which was unlocked, and Morgana opened it, finding wooden stairs leading downwards.

"You don't need to come with me if you don't want to."

"I think I have to. I've put everything I've got into this venture, and if there's a chance of being able to move the ghost along, then I'm in."

Morgana gave her back a reassuring pat. "We'll get to the bottom of this, I promise."

"The ghost problem or the stairs?" Rhiannon half-heartedly joked, looking nervously over her shoulder as they began to go down the narrow steps.

The storeroom below was chilly, with stone walls on all four sides. There were no windows as they were below ground level now, but the room was well lit by a single bulb shining a bright white. The room was empty apart from about twenty cardboard boxes which had obviously been stacked in a pile but were now thrown far and wide, many on their sides with their contents spilling out onto the dusty concrete floor.

Morgana looked around, but again saw no sign of a ghost.

"I stacked them against that wall." Rhiannon pointed to the far side of the room, now the only space totally clear of boxes. She gave a noise of distress and picked up a book from near her feet, cradling it to her chest.

"These are all second-hand books, and some of them are really old and special."

"Then let's get them back in their boxes," Morgana said, stooping to set a box the right way up and neatly putting the books back inside.

"Oh, you don't need to do that." Rhiannon also began to pick up all the books. "I can do it myself, only I don't really want to be down here on my own. It has a creepy vibe, don't you think?"

"It's no trouble. I don't have anything else on today anyway. I think the creepy vibe is because this room's underground. There must have been a tunnel in the cliff here, and it was widened to make this storeroom. The whole peninsula is riddled with them, bored out by streams that dried up centuries ago." She chatted conversationally as she collected up the books.

"There's nothing at all under my shop, but Pixie's Place over the road once had a tunnel connecting it to the premises next door. It was big enough to walk right from one building to the next but was filled in with cement a long time ago. They are closer to the cliff edge than you and it could have undermined the structural integrity of the cliff or something like that."

They filled the boxes, neatly restacking them in their original place.

When they were done, they stood back to admire their efforts and Morgana dusted off her hands on her skirt. "There, that's b…"

She broke off as a wind came out of nowhere and began to circle the room.

Rhiannon let out a squeak, clutching at Morgana's arm.

The wind picked up strength and blew harder and harder until it concentrated on the back wall, blasting all the boxes they'd just restacked back into the middle of the room.

Once more, their contents were scattered.

Morgana put her hands on her hips.

"Well, that's just childish!" she admonished the room.

"Do you see the ghost?" Rhiannon asked in a whisper.

"No, I'm still not sure it's a ghost actually; it's abnormally powerful if it is, but I'm not reading any gathered energy either to suggest a poltergeist. I should be able to feel it if it was. Let me try calling on the only person I can think of that it could be."

Morgana raised her voice. "Valeria Dawson, show yourself. I am Morgana Emrys, and I wish to commune with you."

There was an odd popping noise, then the ghostly figure of a woman materialised in front of Morgana. She was in her late forties, dressed in trainers, green combat trousers and a lime-green tank top. A colourful scarf was tied around her neck and she had multiple piercings in each ear. A tattoo of an ivy vine curled around one bicep.

Her bleached blonde hair was cut short.

"Ow." The ghost rubbed at her temples. "How did you do that?"

"Because I'm a witch." Morgana's mouth tipped up at one side. "Valeria Dawson, I presume?"

"She's here?" Rhiannon looked all around, clearly unable to see the ghost.

"The one and only, and *abnormally powerful* apparently?" Valeria's ghost did a twirl and looked decidedly smug. "So, the stories about your family being witches were true?" Valeria asked. "I must have known your great-great-grandmother or something I think! Lovely lady, she painted landscapes."

"That's my mother," Morgana said, giving Valeria an odd look. "You do realise you've only been dead ten years or so?"

Valeria looked surprised. "Really? Then my husband is still alive?"

"Yes, if Archie Dawson was your husband, then he still lives in Portmage," Morgana said.

Rhiannon tugged on Morgana's arm.

"Archie Dawson is my landlord, I leased this building off him."

Valeria's expression switched to annoyed. "In that case, why hasn't he been to see me?"

"Um, I'm not sure. He probably can't see ghosts?" Morgana said. "You don't know how you died then?"

"Something fell on me from behind. I just remember pain…pain *here.*" She touched the back of her head. "But Archie would have found me, wouldn't he?"

"You were never found. I heard you just vanished."

Valeria's eyebrows shot up. "Then it wasn't an accident?" She put a finger to her nose, tapping it pensively. "I never really thought about it before, but something hit me from behind and it knocked me out. I thought maybe something fell on me and it was just bad luck. But you're suggesting it was murder, aren't you? Is Archie the one that did me in?"

Morgana looked at Rhiannon. "Ghosts are often very confused. They don't really have any sense of time, but it seems Valeria here also didn't realise she was murdered."

"How do you know it was murder?" Rhiannon asked.

"Because she disappeared. She says something hit her knocking her unconscious, but if it was an accident, then someone would have found her body."

"Yes, and now he has a guilty conscience," Valeria put in. "Why isn't he in prison?"

"I don't know the full story, but I expect there wasn't enough evidence to convict him. But how can you be sure it was him if you don't remember anything other than being knocked out?"

"Because he was a lying cheat, always flirting with someone, a real ladies' man. Mostly it was just his way, but I could feel him losing interest in me. I knew there was someone else, someone he liked."

Morgana took a step back as Valeria's anger created more wind to blow around her. She was having trouble pinning down exactly what kind of person Valeria was, especially as she had absolutely no aura at all as a ghost.

She seemed forthright and confident in her stance and her dress, yet definitely insecure when it came to her husband. But perhaps she had good reason to be.

"What's she saying?" Rhiannon asked. "Is she going to keep wrecking the books, and am I in danger? Because it would be good to know."

"And I want to know how long I have to put up with yet another stranger in my business!" Valeria shot back.

Morgana gave Valeria a speculative look. "Do you think we might come to some kind of deal, Valeria? I might be able to help you."

Valeria looked mutinous but only said, "Like what?"

Morgana spread her hands. "Well, it seems obvious to me that you died here because your ghost is here. However, I think it must have been murder because your body wasn't found. It was most likely dumped over the cliffs into the sea and taken away by the tide.

"How would it be if I started looking into the circumstances around your disappearance? I've helped the police on a few murder investigations before and can sometimes use my magical abilities to discover the murderer before the police do. If we found that person and proved it was them, then your spirit could move on?"

"Which might take forever, seeing as you say it's already been ten years," Valeria said.

"True, but in the meantime, I could also try to help you move on through other means. I've had some success with cleansings before, and I'd be willing to try if you were willing to go? It has to be a mutual process or it won't work."

"I'll think about it." Valeria looked sulky. "And what do you want in return?"

"I want you to let Rhiannon here open her bookshop without you interfering."

Rhiannon made a gulping sound.

"You mean I should open the shop even with the

ghost still here?"

"Yes, if Valeria is willing to play nicely with others?"

Morgana shot Valeria a questioning glance.

Valeria pouted. "People means noise, stamping about, making mess."

"You're the one making most of the mess."

Morgana looked pointedly at the books on the floor. She softened her tone.

"Come on, it must be lonely here. Wouldn't it be nicer to have a bit of life going on around you rather than drifting about on your own, scaring everyone away? A bookshop would be a great place to hang out, and it would give you plenty to read to pass the time, at least. Especially as it looks as though you're strong enough mentally to turn the pages?"

"Yes, I am. Is that something most ghosts can't do?"

Morgana grinned and shook her head. "I've never seen a ghost with as strong a will as you've got. Is it true you wrote rude messages on the wall in nail varnish?"

Valeria smiled broadly at this. "I did, I told them to go or I'd make their hair fall out. Cheap fake hair one of them had, *extensions* she called it.

"That nail varnish smelled revolting too. But I suppose I can tolerate a bookshop. There's a few books I always meant to read and never got around to."

She looked down and shifted some of the books on the ground beneath her.

Rhiannon took a step back as she saw them move.

Valeria selected a copy of The Great Gatsby then floated away up the stairs with it, presumably to find a more congenial place to read.

Rhiannon watched the book go up the stairs, held by

an invisible hand, and let out a long breath. "Are you serious, Morgana? You think I'm safe with her here?"

"She's just a person, but she's angry about being dead before her time, which is understandable. Though I do get the feeling she may have been rather assertive in life too. But I think if she agrees to be nice, then you don't have anything to fear."

"But you're going to try to help her move on?"

"Yes, I'll try a cleansing ritual to help her pass over, but the problem is she might be tied here until her murderer is caught."

"You really think you might be able to work out who that is? Even after all this time?" Rhiannon didn't look convinced.

"Maybe. I have a few connections with the local police, so I can at least find out what they know about what happened when she went missing, and I can go and talk to her husband. If he did it, then I might be able to see it; murder sometimes leaves a mark on people.

"In the meantime, why don't we restack these boxes, *again*, and then we'll go and make sure she's on board before I leave, okay?"

Rhiannon gave a weak smile. "Okay, I guess I could always rebrand as a haunted bookshop; you never know, it might even be a selling feature to get customers in."

Chapter Six

Twenty minutes later, Morgana and Rhiannon went back up to the shop floor and found Valeria settled on a large, cracked leather sofa in the bay front of the window.

"That floating book is going to freak people out," Rhiannon commented.

"Valeria? Do you think you could read somewhere more private when customers are here?" Morgana asked the ghost. Valeria grunted, which Morgana took to mean yes. "And are you going to behave yourself and let Rhiannon run her business without interference?"

"Actually," Rhiannon said, "I've been thinking it wouldn't be so bad if Valeria wanted to do a little bit of ghost stuff here and there. Maybe move things just a little, but perhaps not in front of any children. I wouldn't want to scare them. But a haunted bookshop could be a real draw, especially in a village like Portmage with all its magical history around Merlin and King Arthur."

Valeria looked up. "I could do that; it would be fun."

"She agrees to your terms," Morgana told Rhiannon, who looked delighted and immediately set about tearing open one of the boxes of brand new books that would be placed onto the fitted shelves.

"I suppose I'll have to ring the carpenter to come back and repair that fallen bookcase."

"Sorry," Valeria said. "I was just trying to scare you away."

Morgana picked up some of the remains of the scarf scattered on the shop counter and waved them at Valeria. "This kind of pettiness has to stop too; why did you cut up her scarf?"

Valeria looked curiously at the scraps of scarf and then down at the one around her neck. "It's the same as mine. Funny, I don't remember wearing this, I'm not a scarf person."

"Is that why you cut hers up?"

"Actually, I didn't. It wasn't me." Valeria met Morgana's eyes as though to express the truth of her words.

"Then who was it? You must have seen? Unless… do you go anywhere else as well?"

Valeria tugged at the scarf around her neck, looking confused and thoughtful. "I don't go anywhere else, but when evil comes in I can't be here either. It's like being nowhere, I suppose. Sometimes, it's definitely a different day when I return, but I don't know for how long I was gone."

Morgana frowned over this. "What kind of evil?"

Valeria shrugged. "I can't really describe it. It looks like a sort of black cloud. I can feel it when it's near and I leave."

"Has this happened often?"

"I don't know." Valeria looked annoyed by the question and focussed on her novel, so Morgana let it go.

"It's all okay now, can we be friends?" Rhiannon looked between Morgana and the sofa.

"As long as Morgana holds up her end of the bargain to try to find out who my killer was," Valeria said, flipping a page on the book.

"Good, then it's a deal. I'll go and give a friend of mine a call and find out what the police know, and I'll report back when I have something." Morgana left the two of them to it, glad to see Rhiannon seemed comfortable with the ghost and hoping the ghost in question would be nice!

Morgana had butterflies in her stomach as she placed the call to Tristan. She had his direct phone number after being involved in more than one murder case, and she felt it more appropriate to call him directly rather than go through the official police process to report the presence of the ghost. This was because Tristan would understand, whereas the police as a unit might just think she was nuts. Tristan had grown up in Portmage, he'd gone to the same school as she had, and dated her sister for a while. So he knew all about the magic she and her sisters possessed and was completely comfortable with it, having been brought up thinking it was perfectly normal for her family to be witches.

What was particularly unusual about Tristan though, was he'd been such a bad boy heartbreaker when he was young, and now he was an upstanding officer of the law. A Detective Sergeant in fact. He'd left Portmage at the age of eighteen in a puff of motorbike smoke, only to reappear twelve years later as a police detective when Ellie had found a body stuffed in the walk-in fridge of her bakery.

Morgana had been smitten with Tristan when she was a teenager, and she'd never quite been able to shake the crush, but she hoped it didn't show too badly. Especially as she'd met Oliver now. Oliver might very well turn out to be the King Arthur type of man she'd always hoped to find, noble and true. Her taste in men had always been dreadful and she really hoped she'd had a change of luck at last, but then again, he had yet to call her for another date and it might be a bad idea to get her hopes up about the future of their relationship.

"Hello?" Tristan's voice shook her out of her thoughts and the butterflies redoubled inside her. Everything about Tristan reminded her of chocolate. The smoothness of his voice, the colour of his hair and his eyes. Melted chocolate.

She took a deep breath, trying to push the feelings away. "It's me, Morgana."

"Oh no, who is it this time?" His resigned words made her frown.

"What do you mean?" she asked, feeling annoyed.

"Morgana, you only call me when there's murder afoot. So, I'll ask again. Who died?"

"I might be calling socially," she said, nettled.

"Are you?"

"Well, no," she conceded.

He sighed. "Do I need to send out a team to a crime scene?"

"No. It's an old case actually. Have you got anything on a Mrs. Valeria Dawson?"

"You must know I can't discuss any on-going investigations with you, Morgana."

She could hear him tapping keys in the background as he spoke.

"Hmm. Actually, in this case, I can. The investigation was closed years ago. Valeria Dawson disappeared, her body was never found and her sister had her legally declared 'presumed dead' after the usual seven years had elapsed. Have you discovered something about her disappearance?"

"Well, only that she's definitely dead. Her ghost is haunting one of the buildings on Portmage High Street."

She could almost hear Tristan sit up straight at this news. "Murdered?"

"Yes. She says she was hit from behind, but she doesn't remember anything else. If it was just an accident, then why wasn't her body found?"

There was a pause as Tristan read more notes on the case. "Her husband was questioned in connection with the disappearance. It seems he might have been having an affair, and had no alibi for the night she disappeared, but there was also some evidence she was the one having the affair and she'd left him for another man. Apparently, an ex-boyfriend who lived abroad had been exchanging emails with her, and her husband said she'd threatened to leave him for the ex several times. He produced the emails which were enough to cast doubt on her death."

"Well, she didn't and she's definitely dead. So, you might want to think about revisiting that theory? Plus, isn't it also a motive? The jealous husband?" Morgana felt angry on Valeria's behalf that her husband had made her out to be the cheat after he'd probably killed her.

Tristan blew out another breath. "The problem is, Morgana, I can't reopen the case on the basis you've seen her ghost. Real police require real evidence of a murder before we start investigating again."

"But you *know* I can see ghosts."

"And I'd look like a prize idiot if I submitted *that* as evidence to reopen the case! I know you're telling me the truth, but my Detective Inspector is going to need more than your word on it, or mine either."

Morgana drummed her fingers, wondering how to proceed. "Don't you think it's odd her sister was the one to have her declared dead?" she asked.

"No, it was an inheritance situation. She tried to have Valeria declared dead not long after she first disappeared. Their mother was unwell and she didn't want Valeria's husband to have her half of their mother's estate. If Valeria was already legally dead when the mother died, then her sister, Maud, was entitled to all of it."

"But she failed to have her declared dead before the seven years?"

"Yes. But it seems the mother only died six months before the seven years were up and Maud managed to delay the probate from going through until after she had the Certificate of Presumed Death. A court can then decide whether to date it from the application at seven years, or to back date it to the time of the disappearance. Maud Calgary had it backdated so she legally inherited all her mother's estate. Valeria's husband would have been entitled to contest it, but he didn't."

"Does that suggest a guilty conscience? Maybe he already knew she was dead and that he wasn't legally entitled to half her mother's money? He probably didn't want to bring the disappearance back up," Morgana said.

Tristan made a non-committal sound. "Maybe. But it's more likely he didn't want the legal wrangle. Trying to get his share of his wife's inheritance *after* her sister had already gone ahead and had her declared dead *and* proceeded with probate, would have been a long and costly battle. It's more likely he just decided to let it go."

"So, you simply closed the case once she was declared 'Presumed dead'? That doesn't seem right."

"It's because she was only missing, Morgana. If we'd known she'd actually been murdered, then the case would never have been closed. It just becomes a cold case and those are reviewed every two years until someone is found guilty."

"Humph, well, she *was* murdered."

"And I've already told you I can't do anything about it just because you can see her ghost. Get me some evidence and then I can get involved, but until then…"

"Fine, I will," Morgana snapped. "I made a promise to Valeria to help her find peace. Can I have a copy of the missing person file?"

"You can just request it through the Freedom of Information Act, you know?"

Tristan sounded as peevish as she felt, but then relented.

"Very well, I'll make you a copy, but you have to promise me to be cautious, okay? If she was murdered, then the killer is still out there somewhere and might not take too kindly to you poking around."

"Thank you, Tristan," Morgana said sweetly, deliberately avoiding making him any promises.

Chapter Seven

As it was only mid-afternoon by the time Morgana had hung up the phone after her call with Tristan, she decided to strike while the iron was hot and see if Valeria's husband was at home. Ellie had told her roughly where he lived, and as the village wasn't that large, she set out on foot, confident she'd be able to find someone to ask for more precise directions when she was closer.

The wind was beginning to blow as she turned into Crook Lane, and Morgana was regretting her lack of layers, so she decided to start at the far end, where the village met the fields and work her way back until she found Archie Dawson. Sod's Law dictated if she started at the first house then he'd live in the last, so she started with the last one just to be contrary. Lights were on inside, despite it being only 3pm, but the scudding clouds made the sky brooding and lights were being switched on in every house on the lane.

Her knock was answered by a middle-aged man whom she'd seen now and then in the newsagents collecting a paper in the mornings, just as she did herself. They were on nodding terms, though she didn't know his name.

"Hi, so sorry to bother you, I was just wondering if you knew Archie Dawson?"

He gave a wry smile. "Alas, I do know him, he is my constant burden and my greatest enemy."

Morgana opened her mouth to automatically apologise when she caught the humour in his eyes. "Oh, I see. You mean you're Archie Dawson?"

"For my sins."

She raised her eyebrows at this turn of phrase, as she'd essentially come to accuse him of murder. But it was very hard to imagine the man in front of her murdering anyone. He looked like a history teacher, sort of bumbling but charming. He'd probably been very handsome in his youth, but he'd gone to seed now. A small paunch, and white hairs protruding from his ears, made him distinctly non-threatening. There were badly sewn patches on his woollen jumper, and the glasses perched on his forehead were cloudy with fingerprints. She judged him to be in his mid-fifties, and probably hadn't remarried.

Morgana opened up her senses and saw his aura flare into life around him. Healthy, but tinged with a colour she'd normally associate with depression.

"I was wondering if I could have a chat with you about your wife."

He looked surprised, stunned even, but then his arms crossed defensively over his chest.

"Who sent you? Maud? Or are you a reporter?"

"No one sent me exactly. I'm a friend of Rhiannon Lebeau, the lady who's rented the shop premises on the High Street."

"She signed a six-month lease. If she's heard rumours then let me assure you they are nothing but rumours," he said.

Morgana saw tiredness pass over his aura. He was tired of the whole situation. It obviously wasn't the first time the past had caused him problems with leasing the property, but did he know about the ghost? She tried to weigh up how dangerous he might actually be and decided he wasn't.

"Can I come in?"

His shoulders seemed to slump a little more. "Yes, of course. Please do." He stepped back, opening the door wider. As she stepped into the light from his hallway, she saw recognition in his eyes. "I know you, don't I?"

She nodded. "I'm Morgana, and I own Merlin's Attic. I don't think you've ever been in, but I see you passing sometimes."

He looked even more confused but gestured her down the hall and she walked towards the room at the far end, entering into a kitchen-diner.

"Tea?" Archie said.

"Lovely, thank you." Morgana seated herself at his table. She watched while he boiled the kettle and put teabags into mugs, waiting until he'd finished and brought both mugs to the table before she began.

"I'm sorry to just drop in like this, but have you had any complaints before about your property being haunted?"

He heaved a long-suffering sigh. "Yes, several. The place has been nothing but a burden for years. At first, I thought people were looking for a reduction on the rent, and I have actually reduced it several times over the years, but still no one stays there long. It's so ridiculous though. I've had workmen go in and search for drafts or something else that could be causing things to fall over, like uneven flooring, but they've charged me a fortune and apparently done nothing. I think those girls who ran the beauty salon were playing mean pranks on each other. I mean, seriously, a ghost told them to leave?"

"Have you actually been there yourself?" Morgana asked.

"No. I own several buildings; most are in Camelford, and there's always some problem or another to contend with, but that one in particular has been the worst, which is typical as it's the only one I don't really want to go near. It was my wife's place you see, and her dream to open the business, not mine. So, since she left, I avoid the place."

"Except she hasn't left," Morgana said, bluntly. "She's still there, in spirit."

Archie gave her a long look. "Are you being metaphorical?"

"No, sorry. Her ghost is there and she's the one causing the problems."

"Her ghost. Right. I think you've wasted enough of my time, don't you? Why don't you tell me what you really want and then we can both get on with our day?"

He stood up, indicating the interview was over.

"Mr. Dawson, I'm being quite sincere. I've been there myself and I've seen her ghost. If you didn't kill her, then haven't you always wondered what actually happened to her?" Morgana said, not budging.

"She left. She packed her clothes and her passport, and she left me for another man. Her vanishing like that has brought me nothing but pain, so I find your questions in the worst taste. Now, if you don't mind, will you please leave."

He loomed rather menacingly over her, but Morgana refused to be cowed by it.

"Wait, just one more point. Do you remember what she was wearing the night she disappeared? Because I can describe it perfectly."

He sat down again into the chair with a thump. "I do remember, but anyone can ask for the police report and get those details."

"Not the same as actually seeing her though. She was wearing trainers but did the police report also mention the fact there were spots of yellow paint on one of them. She has four earrings in her left ear, one is a dove, one's a green stone, I can't remember the third, but the last one is dangling almost to her shoulder and it's a spiral design. Her hair is short blonde and spiked upwards, but there's a bit at the front that's longer and she blows it off her face. Her…"

"Stop. Who told you all that?" Archie looked wide-eyed.

"No one. I told you, I've seen her for myself."

"It's not possible… She… She's really dead then?"

Morgana didn't reply; she just raised one eyebrow, waiting to see what else he'd say.

Archie stared into his tea. "I thought she must be. She wouldn't have let Maud take all her money like that if she'd been around to prevent it because they hated each other. Val was a strong woman though, independent, free-spirited. So different to me in every way. I've no idea why she married me, I bored her completely, so it wasn't such a stretch to believe she'd simply run off one night."

"I've spoken with her; she gave me the impression you were the one bored of her. She suggested you might have been looking elsewhere?" Morgana didn't want to come right out and accuse him of cheating on his wife as Valeria had.

"No. It wasn't the happiest of marriages, but I was always faithful. There were old letters though, and emails between her and a past boyfriend. I gave them to the police, so they'd know I was telling the truth when I said it was possible she'd just left me."

Morgana watched him critically as he gave a good performance of an abandoned husband, but something in his story just didn't add up.

"Did you really think she might come back? Is that why you weren't the one who had her declared dead?"

"No. I didn't think she'd come back, though it was always there as a possibility, but I didn't particularly want her back either! I certainly didn't want her filing for divorce and taking half my money, but I didn't want her to be dead. Did she say what happened to her?"

Morgana narrowed her eyes, trying to assess if he was worried about what Valeria might have told her. His aura came more into focus, and she saw something unexpected.

He was genuinely sad. But sad about Valeria or sad for himself? It didn't mean he wasn't the one who killed her, but it did mean he had been telling the truth that he didn't want her to be dead. Perhaps the stigma of a vanishing wife had taken more of a toll on his life than he'd anticipated. There must have been whispers following him around. But it was almost odd he hadn't moved away as many people would do in his situation. Start over somewhere new where no one knew anything about your past. But there was also a hint of yellow at the edges of his aura; something he'd said had been a lie, not a big lie, but definitely not the whole truth. She would have to think over the conversation again later and work it out.

"No. She doesn't remember anything more than being hit over the head. So, you stood to lose a fair amount of money if she'd lived?"

He gave a small laugh. "Look around you, I'm far from rich. I do own a few properties, and they're my retirement fund, as it were, so I don't want to lose them. But it's not worth killing over. Val's business was actually doing quite well. The shop was in a prime location on the route to the castle, which is the only reason I haven't sold the dratted place, and we made a decent living from it. She ran the store, and I did the books and the ordering and so on. I'd have been much better off financially if she'd stayed. I mean if she'd lived. But I'm not driven by money, I just want to grow my vegetables and be left in peace. If you're looking for a financial motive then you should meet Maud, Val's sister. She's the one who tried to have her declared dead almost from the moment she went missing. She couldn't stand the thought of me taking any of her mother's money on Val's behalf, which I was legally entitled to as her husband."

"And did you?" Morgana asked, even though she already knew the answer. She just wanted to hear what he'd say.

"I never even tried. I didn't want it. I'm comfortable and it's enough."

"But if Valeria had returned, wouldn't she be annoyed you let her sister take the lot?"

He gave a shrug. "She could have claimed it once she'd been through the process of coming back from the dead. It's not as though Maud would have spent it as she's the most tight-fisted person on the planet, just wants money for money's sake."

"Do you know where I can find her?" Morgana asked.

"She volunteers at the charity shop in Wadebridge, the big one on the corner of South Street."

"That sounds pretty altruistic," Morgana said, thinking someone who gave up their time to work in a charity shop must be nicer than he was making out.

He gave another mirthless laugh. "She does it so she doesn't have to buy clothes, or books, or DVDs. She gets first pick of everything coming in. She's always dressed in the most elegant clothes because she snaffles the very best of the donations before they even reach the shelves. It's her way of getting everything for next to nothing. I'm telling you, she's a Scrooge-level miser. She can have Val's half of the money and I hope it brings her some joy. Now, if you don't have any more questions, I'd really like some space to think. The fact my wife is haunting her old shop is kind of a big one to get my head around."

"Of course, thank you for the tea." Morgana got to her feet and followed him back towards the front door, only pausing as she spotted a box in the hallway where a length of material could be seen coming out of the top.

"Oh. This looks familiar." She bent to look more closely. The material was a gold satin, shot through with glitter that gave an impression of starlight.

"Those?" Archie stopped and pulled the protruding scarf from the box. "They're left over from Val's business. I meant to order five of them and accidentally ended up with a box of fifty. I've been giving them as birthday presents to various relatives ever since."

"Valeria's ghost is wearing one of these," Morgana said, remembering where she'd seen it. "And you gave one to Rhiannon Lebeau too, right?"

His brow furrowed. "Yes, I gave one to Ms Lebeau, but are you sure Val has one on? She didn't really like them, it's not her style."

"That's odd." Morgana was talking more to herself now than him. "This is the same scarf as Rhiannon's that was cut to pieces. We thought Valeria did it, but she claimed she didn't. I wonder…" Her voice trailed off as she realised Archie was looking at her as though she would never leave when he'd clearly had enough.

"I appreciate your time, Mr. Dawson, and I'm sorry for your loss." She went past him and out of the door.

She wasn't convinced he was Valeria's murderer, but she also wasn't convinced he was completely innocent either. He'd definitely lied at some point during their conversation.

Also, the murder was so long ago now, he could well be over the violence it had taken to commit and that would explain why it hadn't shown at all in his aura.

But for now, she had a new lead to follow. She decided she'd get someone to cover her shop for one day in the week and she'd go to Wadebridge to question Val's sister, Maud.

Chapter Eight

Morgana was exceedingly impressed with herself for having the foresight to ring the charity shop and find out what days Maud volunteered there, and it was with this information in hand that she didn't set out for Wadebridge until Thursday. Parking wasn't a problem during the low season, and she secured a place almost right outside, which was just as well as it had begun to rain heavily.

She stopped in surprise for a moment outside, seeing a woman hanging Christmas lights in the window and realised with a start it was the first of December. A frisson of excitement went through her. Christmas was an excellent time of the year in retail, but it meant so much more than that to most people; they were kinder, warmer in personality, and altogether more cheerful in the run up to the festivities. Morgana liked seeing people happy.

Her mother and Ellie usually laid on Christmas jointly, with Ellie's children running riot and Morgana and Morwenna bickering and cackling like the two witchy aunts they were.

Of course, Morwenna had recently got engaged, which might change things, but as it was Morwenna's fourth engagement, she suspected it wouldn't. She also briefly wondered if she and Oliver might still be an item by then? But he still hadn't called to arrange a second date, so perhaps not.

Pushing that thought quickly aside, she opened the door to the charity shop and stepped inside.

"Hello love, sorry, I can't move, this bit's tricky," the

woman in the window called out. "Maud?" She raised her voice to a shout and Morgana turned round to see a second woman emerge from the door at the far end. Her hopes sank a little as she examined Maud. She'd hoped she was the plump cheerful woman in the window, but instead, she now knew she was the other one. Stick thin with a pinched face as if she'd been sucking lemons, Maud looked annoyed at having to serve a customer.

"It's fine," Morgana said, "I'm just browsing." She wandered over to a rack of women's dresses and began to flick through them. Maud glowered at her and Morgana chewed her lip, wondering how to get this unfriendly woman to start talking.

She held up a dress in an inky blue and turned towards a long mirror to see if it would suit her. "What do you think?" she asked.

Maud sniffed, as though unimpressed. "I think you could use a little more colour. Your clothes are very dark. How about the pink one?" She pointed to an extremely ugly pink dress with shoulder pads and Morgana eyed it doubtfully.

"I'm not a big fan of pink," she said. "I prefer stronger colours."

"A nice red scarf would cheer your look up a bit." Maud pointed to a wire basket filled with scarves, which Morgana eyed thoughtfully. Scarves seemed to be a theme recently for some reason. Rhiannon in her many scarves of various colours that she dropped wherever she went. Valeria in the gold satin scarf. Rhiannon's gold satin scarf that had been cut to shreds. Valeria denying she had done it... Morgana wanted to think about it some more, but this wasn't the time. She walked over to the wire basket and began to sort through them.

"Red would certainly be very seasonal, but perhaps something in gold would do just as well?" She gave a side-glance at Maud as she said it to see if her comment elicited any kind of reaction. All she got was another sniff of disapproval.

"Your rings and bracelets are all silver," Maud said. "Are you sure gold is really the right colour for you?"

"Oh, good point, very observant," Morgana replied, deciding she'd be better off just getting straight to the point. "You're Valeria's sister, aren't you?"

Maud's gaze turned even colder at these words, and her head tilted with an unspoken question.

"I'm from Portmage," Morgana explained, "so I'm familiar with the mystery of her disappearance. People still talk about it, and her husband still lives there."

Maud made a sound of exasperation. "It's not a mystery, her husband murdered her."

"You don't think there's any chance at all she decided to leave him?"

"Pah, she wouldn't have walked away without her share of their properties. She was entitled to half. All this nonsense about a boyfriend abroad—he's just covering his tracks. Not that I wouldn't have put it past her to vanish and then reappear just to spite me. She loved making waves and making my life as difficult as possible. It was an absolute pain to have her declared dead, and expensive too."

"You didn't hold out any hope she might come back?" Morgana was slightly shocked at how unfeeling Valeria's sister was. She regularly found her own sister irritating beyond belief, but she'd never have her declared dead if there were any chance at all of her still being alive somewhere.

"Oh, I knew she was dead. I hired a medium and checked. Valeria herself told me she'd been murdered."

Morgana's brows shot up. "Really?"

"The police wouldn't listen though; apparently, they don't respect the words of a medium."

Seeing as Morgana herself had already told a member of the police force she'd seen Valeria's ghost, and had been basically ignored, she had to be sympathetic on this point.

"Did Valeria say who had killed her?"

"Not directly; the dead don't speak all that coherently. She gave clues, but I worked out they meant that no-good husband of hers. Archie Dawson was a philanderer. I expect he's married that barmaid now, she was the most persistent of his mistresses, always dropping in after Val's disappearance. I couldn't speak to him about the situation without tripping over that woman. I warned Val not to marry such a good-looking man. They're never faithful." Maud crossed her arms as though that were her last word on the subject.

Morgana regarded Maud with mixed feelings. On the one hand, she knew darn well ghosts could be perfectly coherent, and the giving of clues suggested the Medium was probably a fraud. Yet at the same time, she was grappling with the idea of Archie Dawson as a good-looking man. Maud wasn't the first to say so, and Valeria herself had said the same. But the Archie she'd met had obviously gone to seed. Maud's bitterness towards him was interesting too, and Morgana got the feeling Maud might rather Archie had married her instead.

"Which barmaid?" Morgana said, fishing for further information.

"Some money-grabber from the local pub, but I made sure everyone knew it was him. Smart women don't chase a man who has murdered his wife, do they? Not unless they want to end up the same way. Now, did you want to buy something?"

Morgana knew she wouldn't get much more from Maud, who had begun tapping her foot. So, she quickly selected the red scarf and purchased it, thinking she could give it to her nephew for decorating a snowman if it snowed this winter.

On the drive back to Portmage, Morgana thought over what Maud had said. Maud was convinced Valeria was dead, but had she really believed it just because a medium told her so?

She didn't seem the type to believe in the supernatural, and Morgana had to wonder if she'd either made the story up or only sought the help of a medium to get some kind of proof to advance her own situation. Not that it counted as proof, as Maud had found out, and surely, she must have known it wouldn't? If Morgana hadn't been sure Tristan would believe what she was saying, then she'd never have even told him about seeing Valeria's ghost. Not that it had done her any good either.

Perhaps she should have asked who the medium was, and paid her a visit herself? She quickly dismissed this idea. She could go straight to the source and ask Valeria if she'd ever been summoned, and that would resolve the question as to the medium's credentials. With this in mind, Morgana parked her car around the back of her own premises and then walked the few hundred meters along the High Street to Lebeau Books. The business wasn't officially open yet, but she could see Rhiannon through the window, stacking books into shelves and apparently talking to herself. She knocked on the glass, and her new friend smiled with pleasure at the sight of her.

"Come in, Morgana, it's lovely to see you." Rhiannon greeted enthusiastically.

"How are you getting on?" Morgana asked.

"Going a bit stir-crazy. I've not really spoken to another soul since you left unless you count my ghost. I find myself talking to her instead and I'm sure she's sick to death of my prattling."

"Sick to death?" Valeria chuckled at the unintended pun from the sofa where she was stretched out relaxing. "I don't mind it, it's company. Plus, I can call her rude things and she doesn't know."

"That's only because she can't hear you," Morgana admonished.

"She can't?" Rhiannon said.

"Oh, I wasn't talking to you, I was talking to Valeria. Sorry, this is going to get confusing! Is it going okay, having her here?"

"Oh yes, she's been fine, unless you count the upset in the basement again. Remember all those boxes she chucked about, then we restacked them and she messed them up again?"

"I remember," Morgana said. "We restacked them for a third time and she promised to stop being annoying."

"Yes, well, she knocked them down again."

Morgana turned and glared at Valeria. "Seriously?"

Valeria shrugged uncaringly.

Morgana blew out a frustrated breath. "Do you want me to help tidy them?"

"No, it's okay," Rhiannon said. "I moved them to the other side of the room and since then, she's let them be. She moves books around and makes me jump sometimes when they float past, but I can live with that. Hiding my car keys is a bit of a nuisance though."

"I don't hide them. She's just scatty," Valeria said with an eye roll. "I actually spend a great deal of time locating the damn keys and leaving them on the counter where she can find them."

Morgana repeated this to Rhiannon in slightly nicer words, and Rhiannon gave a rueful smile. "I believe her. I do have a tendency to be rather scatterbrained when I'm thinking of a million things like I have to right now. I'm planning a big opening on Saturday, with Champagne at 6pm, will you come?"

"I wouldn't miss it," Morgana promised. "Valeria, I saw your sister today and she said she'd spoken with you through a medium, do you have any recollection of that?"

Valeria's lip twisted into a disbelieving smirk. "Maud went to a medium? Pull the other one! No, no one's spoken to me in my boring afterlife; I'd remember it."

"I thought it seemed unlikely too," Morgana agreed. "But I had to check. Do you think there's any chance she might have been the one to murder you? She didn't seem very upset about your disappearance, more annoyed really."

"We've never gotten along. She actually introduced

Archie and me; they were neighbours many years ago, and she was really cross when we got together. Wanted him for herself," Valeria said, confirming Morgana's suspicions. "He was bachelor number one in her village. Not that being married stopped women throwing themselves at him, and he was always too nice to snub any of them."

"Maud said there was a barmaid always calling on him after you disappeared. Do you know who she might be?"

"Ugh, that would be Belinda from The Fisherman's Rest. She was at least sixty and had a face like a bag of spanners, but she had a definite soft spot for Archie. He once went over to her house when her water pipe burst as she claimed she didn't know any other men capable of fixing it! She was always leaning over the bar in low-cut tops and pretending to be interested in his talk about his garden. Quite ridiculous the way women fawned over him."

"I went to visit him on Monday after meeting you to see his reaction to the news you were haunting here, and I have to confess, I can't see what the attraction is. He just looks like an average, tired and middle-aged man to me."

"Oh, he was ever so charming though," Rhiannon put in, managing to keep up with Morgana's side of the conversation. "But he did seem rather sad and lonely, as though he was not looking after himself anymore and had let things go a bit."

"I wish I could see him now," Valeria said. "He'll have aged ten years, but I always thought he'd age well."

"If your husband was such a catch," Morgana said,

still struggling to believe it, "then maybe it was a love rival that murdered you?"

Valeria scowled. "If that's the case, then you're going to have an extremely long list of suspects!"

Chapter Nine

On Saturday afternoon, Morgana closed up her shop half an hour early and took a quick shower before going to the bookshop opening. At 6pm in December, it was already dark and most of the businesses on the High Street had already closed, but Lebeau Books was lit up and welcoming. Morgana stopped to admire the window display which featured a Christmas tree made out of a huge stack of books, all wrapped in red and green with gold and silver bows stuck artistically here and there. Inside, she could see people gathered around the coffee table, chatting animatedly on the sofa and the armchairs, while sipping at glasses of Champagne. Rhiannon had done an excellent job at promoting her opening and it was obviously going well.

Morgana went inside and found one of Ellie's waitresses standing there, holding a tray of glasses containing either Champagne or orange juice. Behind the till already madly ringing up purchases was Lily, who helped Morgana out during the summer months and covered for her occasionally when needed.

Rhiannon came rushing over and greeted Morgana enthusiastically. "Can you believe how many people have turned up? They're all saying they've wanted a bookshop for years in Portmage and they're all going to give each other books for Christmas. This is a dream come true for me."

"I join the rest of the village in that sentiment." Morgana grinned at her and handed back the scarf that had dropped at her feet. "Plus, free fizz is always going to make you an instant hit."

Rhiannon laughed. "Not only that, but there's also a reporter here and she was thrilled with the story of a ghost haunting the place. She's going to run a big feature on the bookshop next week and says people will be coming from all over to visit to try to spot something spooky happening." Rhiannon leaned closer and lowered her voice, "Is Valeria about? It might be quite useful if she did something now."

Morgana looked around and spotted Valeria watching the scene rather wistfully from the door to the cellar. "Yes, she's here. I'll go and ask her." Morgana took her Champagne flute and skirted a display table, stopping by the closed stockroom door and pretending to look at the books to one side of it.

"Hello Valeria. Are you enjoying the party or are you finding it all a bit too much?"

"It's a success, isn't it?" Valeria said. "It does make me miss my own little boutique being in this space, but I suppose if it had to be anything else then I'm glad it's a bookshop. Much better than that beauty parlour with all their vile-smelling products."

"I didn't know ghosts could smell?" Morgana said.

"Well, to be honest, until I became a ghost I didn't know any of these things either. But I can certainly smell, and can sense things I couldn't before."

"That's interesting and I'd love to question you more about it at some point. Most of the ghosts I've spoken to in the past have been a lot more disconnected than you, and it's been hard to hold their attention long enough to find this stuff out."

"Actually, I've been meaning to ask you, Morgana; why do you think I'm more powerful than other ghosts you've met? I mean, I know I had a strong personality when I was alive, but I'm not powerful in the way you are as a witch, or anybody particularly special."

"Ghosts are rarer than you'd think, so I haven't had a huge amount of experience, but I'd say it's probably got something to do with your strength of will. It may also have something to do with the way you died. A peaceful death rarely leaves a ghost."

"So what you're saying is it's likely I had a violent death?" Valeria said.

Morgana shifted her position slightly as another book browser gave her a curious look and angled herself away from their view. "I do think you were murdered and I'm trying to solve it. This probably isn't the time or place, but is there anything else you can remember about that night? For example, you said something hit you from behind, but do you remember what time that was or where you were standing?"

Valeria looked around the room thoughtfully, her eyes resting on the far corner. "I was standing about there, hanging earrings onto a display stand that used to be over there, then something fell on top of me and everything went black. That's all I remember. It was late though, dark outside even though it was summer. I remember hearing chimes in the distance from the church, so it was just past eleven at night."

"That's pretty late," Morgana commented. "Wouldn't your husband be worried about the fact you hadn't come home yet?"

"It was a Wednesday, delivery day. If I had a big order coming in, then I'd often be here until past midnight putting it all away and Archie would just go to bed. It's not really so strange he didn't notice I was missing. Of course, he'd know I wasn't coming home if he was the one who came here to murder me, but the more I think about it, the less sense it makes. He was a liar and a cheat, but wasn't exactly the violent type. Why not just ask for a divorce if he'd fallen in love with someone else? I feel more and more it was just an accident."

Morgana turned and looked at the corner where Valeria said she'd been standing. "Do you really think something fell on you? That seems an odd spot to have something behind you big enough to come down and knock you out."

Valeria frowned. "You're right. There was nothing behind me. Just empty space."

"So, what you thought was something falling must have been a person behind you who hit you with something, wouldn't you say? But how did they get in? I'm assuming if it was that late, then the door was locked. Did your husband have a key?"

"Actually," Valeria said slowly. "I don't think the door *was* locked. After all, this is Portmage, there's zero crime here. No one was going to come into a shop with the lights on and someone inside and attempt to steal something. It just doesn't happen here."

"No," Morgana agreed, turning to scan the room. "Stealing doesn't happen much, but murder sometimes does."

"How morbid," Valeria said, tilting a grin at Morgana who had just taken a sip from her glass and discovered it was empty. "This is supposed to be a party, isn't it? And you're standing in a corner talking to a dead person about murder instead of socialising."

Morgana grinned back. "Which is exactly why everyone in the village thinks I'm so weird. In fact, I came over here for a reason, then got distracted. Rhiannon was wondering if you might do a few ghostly things, like move a couple of books, nothing big, but enough to catch the attention of the journalist over there."

"No problem, leave it with me." Valeria rubbed her hands together. "A bit of hocus-pocus coming up."

Morgana turned back to face the party, a random book in her hand, and noticed her sister, Ellie, had come in at some point while she'd been at the back of the room apparently talking to the wall. She returned to the seating area near the front window where Ellie was perching on the arm of a sofa, and the two sisters clinked their glasses in greeting.

"I have a feeling this might outlast the other businesses that have been here," Ellie said. "And I can't say I'm not glad. I like Rhiannon."

"I agree, I think she'll be a good addition to the village. She's a fun person to be around and full of warmth."

"Have you checked her with your third eye?" Ellie asked. "I know you're getting better at seeing auras when you need to and that opening your third eye really takes it out of you, but if she's here to stay, then it might be a good idea to get a proper look at what kind of a person she is underneath?"

Morgana shook her head. "I can't check out every new person I come across. It's still really difficult to do and it makes me completely blind and exhausted for quite a while afterwards, so I try not to use my third eye unless I really have to. Anyway, even though an aura is only a picture of that person's emotions at a precise moment, if people are intrinsically bad, then they tend to carry it with them all the time."

"Can you see the auras in here tonight?" Ellie asked.

"No, with this many people it gets completely overwhelming. Don't forget I also *feel* what I see, and with this many people, it would all get muddled into one big ball of emotions that would swamp me. I've been working on being able to put up a strong mental barrier against crowds, though it's still not as quick to put up or take down as I'd like it to be."

At that moment, a distraction was caused as a book slid out from the top shelf making a woman beneath it let out a yelp as it hit the floor beside her. On the opposite side of the store, another book did the same, but this time made a lazy circle of the room before landing at the feet of the journalist, who had wasted no time in lifting her camera to her face and snapping pictures in rapid succession to capture the action.

Rhiannon spread her arms delightedly in a 'there you go' gesture, then tutted as Valeria tipped over a stand of bookmarks which scattered all over the counter.

"As you can see, ladies and gents, the bookshop is possibly a little bit haunted, but please don't be alarmed as the ghost appears to be friendly and likes to occasionally recommend a book, nothing more."

Morgana saw Valeria roll her eyes with good humour until her expression suddenly darkened and she picked up a book from a display table and hurled it at the shop entrance before vanishing.

All eyes turned to the door just as Archie Dawson came through it, ducking the book and seemingly startled to find everyone staring.

Chapter Ten

"Oh, um, hello." He looked around nervously. There was a small outbreak of whispering and he sighed, his shoulders slumping slightly. "Miss Lebeau? I just wanted to come and wish you luck with the business."

Rhiannon drew him further into the bookshop, tucking her arm in his and making it clear he was welcome and she didn't think he was a killer. Morgana wasn't quite so sure. He'd said something to her she'd known was wrong, but she had yet to work out what it was. She regarded him suspiciously while at the same time looking around for Valeria, but Valeria was gone.

"I brought you a present, well, the *same* present. Your friend mentioned yours was cut up or something?" He held a gold satin scarf out to Rhiannon tentatively, as though not entirely sure she'd want it. But Rhiannon was delighted and immediately added it to the collection already hanging around her neck.

"That's so kind, Mr. Dawson. I was really upset when mine was destroyed." Rhiannon lowered her voice as she continued talking and Morgana surmised she was telling him about Valeria.

He didn't stay long, just enough time to be given a quick tour of the store front and to drink an orange juice. As he turned to go, another woman who'd come in just behind him stopped him by the door.

From the sofa, Morgana watched with interest as she addressed him. "Archie, it's been weeks since I've seen you, are you feeling any better?" The woman was in her thirties, with long tousled curls Morgana envied. She wore a lot of make-up but was undeniably pretty.

"I have good days and bad days, Jen. Today is not great so I'm going home again now but thank you for asking." He gave her a smile almost transforming his face, and Morgana suddenly saw a glimpse of why women found him attractive. She also had to admit he did look rather pale. Quite possibly, this was the first time in years he'd been back to the place that had once been Valeria's boutique.

Mr. Dawson slipped out of the door and the woman watched him go, frowning as she did. After a moment of apparent indecision, she accepted a Champagne flute from Lucy and began to wander around the shop, browsing the books.

"Who is that?" Morgana asked Ellie.

"That's Jennifer Penwyn. She lives in Pixie Cove. Why?"

"She was talking to Archie Dawson. Maybe she was one of his alleged women?"

"Really?" Ellie looked doubtful. "She's a lot younger than Archie, she was probably just being friendly to him. I think she works at the Cliff Hotel. Greg and I went there for a spa day, and I saw her serving the afternoon tea. She used to live in Portmage with an aunt or something, but I haven't seen her in the village for ages. Still, everyone likes books, right?"

"Hmm, I don't suppose you've also seen Belinda, the barmaid from the Fisherman's Rest?"

"I have actually," Ellie said, making Morgana sit bolt upright. "She's by the door."

Morgana instantly spotted Belinda. She knew her by sight, though not to chat to. Morgana's local pub was The Knights at Arms, located in Portmage Village on the top of the cliffs. She rarely had a reason to visit the pub down by the beach, which was a bit of a walk away in Lower Portmage.

"She's staring out of the window after Archie Dawson. Suspicious, don't you think?"

"There could be nothing at all in the rumours, you know," Ellie pointed out in a lecturing tone. "People chat to barmaids and it's part of their job to listen and seem interested."

"Well, I'm going to go and talk to her." Morgana skirted quickly around several shoppers, concerned Belinda would leave before she reached her, and made a point of getting in the woman's way before she could.

"Hello, how lovely to see you," Morgana greeted. She noted the fact Belinda was heavily made up and her clothes were those of a much younger woman, but she had a definite 'barmaid' look about her and a bright smile that was probably a job requirement.

"Hello, Morgana, isn't it?" Belinda gave her a nod of greeting in return.

"That's right. Did I see Archie Dawson just leave?" Morgana couldn't think of a better way of opening the conversation and hoped it would get Belinda talking.

"Yes."

"You're friends, aren't you?"

Belinda gave her a suspicious look. "You could say that. He used to come to the pub a lot, in the old days, before his wife disappeared."

"But not anymore?" Morgana asked.

"Not much, no. I must say I miss him. His presence at the bar always made my night. Such a lovely man. But he changed after his wife left."

"Really?"

Belinda nodded, staring out at the night as though suddenly lost in thought. "He was so cheerful back then, even with his cold-hearted wife always trying to break his spirit. But she never did, he was full of life. Making plans for the future."

"A future with you?" Morgana almost kicked herself for being so obvious, but Belinda didn't seem to notice.

"He never said anything like that, but we had a connection. I know it created some talk. Then Valeria disappeared and he was suddenly living under a cloud of suspicion. He didn't come to the pub anymore. I think he wanted to try and show everyone he had no motive, so he stayed away from me. I did try to convince him he was being stupid. After all, he didn't kill her so there couldn't be any proof against him. He was free to be happy, but he didn't see it that way. He's hiding, you see. Hiding from the world that thinks he's a killer, but he just needs time."

Morgana chewed on the inside of her lip. Ten years was a long time to wait for someone.

"Do you remember the night Valeria went missing?" she asked.

Belinda nodded. "I was working, and we were there until quite late, so I didn't hear about it until the next day. When you work in a pub, you're lucky to get away before midnight."

Morgana absorbed that. It meant Belinda definitely had an alibi for the time of the murder, or was she just saying it because she knew exactly what time Valeria was murdered and wanted to plant the idea of an alibi? It surely wouldn't be that hard for someone to ask to finish early on a particular night? She wondered if the police had ever taken Belinda's statement.

"I must go," Belinda said, her eyes still on the door.

Morgana waved her off, wondering if her haste was because she had to get to work, or if she was actually following Archie.

It was only as she scanned the room, wondering who to speak to next that she noticed once again the woman who'd spoken to Archie before he'd left. She watched Jennifer Penwyn sit down at a table in the middle of the room, two books beside her ready to be purchased, and noticed a flash of gold around her neck. A very familiar gold scarf.

Chapter Eleven

Jennifer began to flick through the books she'd selected, and Morgana plonked herself down beside her.

"Hi, it's Jennifer, isn't it?" Morgana gave the other woman a bright smile.

"Yes, have we met?" Jennifer seemed distracted.

"Maybe, I'm Morgana Emrys, I own a shop here in Portmage."

"Oh, yes. We have met. I used to live in Portmage a long time ago. I remember your dad, such a nice man. I was so sorry to hear what happened to him." Jennifer warmed up considerably.

"Thank you." Morgana didn't want to dwell on it. Her father had been manning the lifeboat during a storm and had been lost at sea when Morgana was twelve years old.

"He used to bring you to The Knights at Arms when you were only about nine years old. Of course, I was barely more than a teenager myself at the time, but he used to make time to say hello as I collected up the glasses. You and your twin were great comedy value, running around the garden making mischief, and your older sister runs the bakery now, doesn't she? I don't get into Portmage often anymore, but when I do, I always stop there for some of her scones."

The bookshop was warm with all the people inside and Morgana wasn't surprised when Jennifer shrugged out of her coat.

"Oh," she said, getting a closer look at the gold scarf around Jennifer's neck. "That's lovely; it looks a bit like the one Mr. Dawson just gave to Rhiannon."

"Yes. He gave this one to me years ago. Poor man." Her voice was full of sympathy.

"Why do you say that?"

"Because everyone thinks he murdered his wife. All thanks to his awful sister-in-law who spread lies to anyone who'd listen. You only have to talk to him to know he didn't, and he's so sad now. If she'd just left him a note or something to say she was leaving, but instead she just vanished and it ruined Archie's life."

"You think she left him? You don't think something happened to her?"

"She packed a suitcase, didn't she?" Jennifer downed the glass and looked around for another. Lucy immediately appeared at her elbow and offered another, which Jennifer took gratefully.

Morgana's eyes widened with realisation. *That* was what was wrong with Archie's story. He said she'd packed her bags and taken her passport, but Morgana knew for a fact Valeria had done no such thing. She'd never even returned home. She had to speak to Tristan immediately. Archie had definitely lied on his statement and that might be enough to reopen the case?

"Yes, of course. If you'll excuse me, I need to make a phone call."

Jennifer put a hand on Morgana's arm, stopping her. "If Valeria was murdered, then I know who did it."

"You do?" Morgana stayed in her seat, all her attention back on Jennifer.

"Definitely. It would have been Bethany Musgrove. She was so obviously in love with Archie and very jealous of him talking to other women. Not that Archie ever encouraged her, but she followed him around all the time. Stalking him in my opinion, always there in the distance. Whenever I went to visit him, I'd see her peering over the hedge in the garden, very sly sort of woman. I felt so sorry for him. I understood his isolation, you see. The village never really accepted him again after that."

Jennifer twisted her fingers together, looking stressed, and Morgana caught a flash of unhappiness on her aura. Being able to see a glimpse of Jennifer's aura, despite Morgana having all her mental blocks in place, meant the emotion must be very strong to penetrate through them. She suddenly felt rather sorry for the woman. She might be beautiful and outwardly content, but she was obviously single and lonely. No wonder she identified with Archie Dawson.

"I hope you find a good book; I find the escapism of fiction a great help," she said, feeling it was a lacklustre suggestion.

"I agree." Jennifer gave a strained smile. "No romance novels for me though, I love dystopian stuff, the end of the world and a quest to save humanity. I think I'll purchase these and get home to spend the evening reading with a nice Pinot noir for company."

Morgana grinned. "Sounds good."

"I'm glad I came though. I'm always interested to see what people do with this place. Did you know it's been quite a lot of different things over the years?"

"Yes, though I have a feeling a 'haunted bookshop' will do very well in Portmage and will outlast the others."

"Haunted?" Jennifer looked horrified. "By whom?"

"No idea," Morgana said, airily. "Maybe Valeria

Dawson?"

Jennifer rose quickly to her feet. "So that's why they all left, all those businesses that were here before. She's still around making everyone's life a misery. As if she hadn't already done enough! It was nice to meet you, anyway."

"Likewise," Morgana said. She stayed at the table for another minute, committing everything Jennifer had said to memory. At least now she had two new leads. Archie *had* lied to the police and there was a new suspect too. Checking out Bethany Musgrove was next on her agenda.

Valeria had been right when she'd said there were a lot of women in Archie's life. Morgana looked around for Valeria again, but there was still no sign of her. Perhaps she was in the basement, upset over seeing her husband again after all this time? Morgana rose to her feet and went over to Rhiannon.

"Would it be okay if I went down to the basement? I'd like a word with Valeria, but she's not here."

"Yes, of course." Rhiannon was perspiring slightly as she moved about the room, helping people find what they wanted and topping up drinks. "Tell her I said thank you."

"Will do. You might want to go and butter up those three old ladies talking to Ellie; they're the matriarchs of the village, and if they like this place, then they'll tell everyone and anyone who'll listen. They could make or break you," Morgana said. "But don't be offended if they quiz you about your love life or if they criticise your clothes, that's just the way they operate."

"Appreciate the warning." Rhiannon tucked a lock

of hair behind her ear and another one of her scarves fell to the floor. "Bother. I think I'll just leave that one there."

Morgana put it on the counter for her and then skirted along one wall, trying to avoid the eyes of the three matriarchs—Mrs. Goodbody, Mrs. Ellington-Jones and Mrs. Braintree, who would corner her and make several passive-aggressive comments if she gave them time to.

All three were widowed and took a great deal of interest in anything that happened in the village. She paused, realising they would also probably be a brilliant source of information on Archie and Valeria and anyone they'd had contact with. Oh well, that would have to wait. First, she wanted to talk to Valeria and then she'd need to call Tristan. Solving a murder that happened years earlier wasn't easy.

"Valeria, are you down here?" Morgana descended the steps into the basement. There was no answer, but she went right down in case Valeria was upset. It was still bare except for the boxes now stacked against the wall on her left instead of at the back, and the single bulb hung depressingly still over the dusty floor.

"Valeria?" she asked, putting a little of her will into the summons.

Valeria appeared, popping through the wall as though against her will. "Oh, it's you."

"Are you okay?"

Valeria thinned her lips. "No."

"Because of Archie being here?"

"I don't know." Valeria paced around the room. "Evil was here, it literally drove me out, Morgana. I saw

Archie at the door and was feeling furiously angry, then it was like I got sucked out of the building! Stuck in a sort of dark limbo until you pulled me back."

"Really? I've not heard of that happening before." Morgana perched on a stack of boxes. "Evil, like someone with power over the dead? Or evil, like maybe your killer had just come in?"

"How should I know? All I know is I couldn't get back and believe me, I tried. I have a few things I wanted to say to that husband of mine. But it was like I'd been banished. So, it wasn't you?"

"It wasn't me, and anyway, I'm not evil," Morgana confirmed.

"No, but it would take someone like you to affect me, wouldn't it?"

"Not necessarily. If Archie was the one who murdered you, then maybe your soul somehow knew and couldn't be here when he was?"

Valeria tapped a finger to her chin. "I suppose that makes sense."

"On the other hand, there were a lot of people coming in around that time, so it could have been any of them. Are you sure you didn't feel anything emanating off anyone in particular?"

"No, but it felt horrid, sort of sticky and vile. I didn't want to leave, but didn't want to stay either. In fact, I've had enough of this ghosting business. I thought you said you were going to help me cross over, but you haven't done anything about it. I just want to move on now."

Morgana held up a placating hand.

"Of course, and I'm sorry I haven't tried yet, but having you around might help with solving your murder.

Don't you want to know who did it?"

"Why should I care? I'm dead either way. Just do your stuff." Valeria folded her arms and glared at Morgana.

"I will, I need to prepare some things first, but I'll do it tomorrow if that's what you want. I can't guarantee success though; necromancy is a tricky business and I'm not very experienced. But please think about staying a little longer. You might be dead but there's still a murderer out there and they might kill again. Helping me could save someone else's life, and your knowledge could be invaluable."

"Humph. I'll think about it, but it could take years at the rate you're going. Have you discovered anything new at all?"

"I'm not sure." Morgana gave a sigh of frustration. "Do you know a woman called Bethany Musgrove?"

"That fat frump? You think she's a suspect? She couldn't murder a spider, let alone me."

"Belinda was here too," Morgana replied.

"Belinda is a tramp. What was she doing here at a bookshop? I expect she can't even read. She probably followed Archie, like a leech."

Morgana hid her smile. Archie certainly had a way of making women all jealous of each other, unintentionally or not.

"I spoke to a woman who suggested Bethany was the one always following Archie; she said she was always peering over the hedge."

"Hardly surprising. The Musgroves' house backs on to ours. She grew a lot of flowers at the bottom of their garden, supplying the local florist. Archie had a vegetable plot at the end of our garden, so they were often chatting over the hedge. But seriously, if you'd met Bethany, you wouldn't suspect her. She's got all the personality of a dormouse. Even her own husband told me she was a total drip. He didn't like her being friendly with Archie though, said Archie was giving her ideas, telling her she could be financially independent with her flower business if she expanded it. He warned me to keep Archie away from her. She's no looker though, not like Belinda, if you like that trashy sort of way she has. I know which one I wouldn't trust. Archie liked strong women. Well, he married me, didn't he?"

"That's true. Do you think there was someone else we haven't considered yet?"

"Maybe. He was a flirt, but he'd never leave me for Belinda or Bethany." She began to pace again, and Morgana suspected she wasn't as sure as she sounded.

"Just one more question. Archie told the police you'd packed your bag and taken your passport. Do you have any memory of doing that?"

"What? No! This business was my life, I worked way too hard building it up to walk away from it. I might have left him one day, but I wouldn't leave Portmage. Why would I need my passport?"

"Why indeed," Morgana said, now sure Archie was involved. "No reason it would be missing except to suggest you left for the ex-boyfriend who lives abroad. But how the heck can I prove it?"

Chapter Twelve

When Morgana closed her doors at 4pm on Sunday afternoon, it was already getting dim outside. She decided to forgo her usual ritual of cleansing the whole space, putting it off until the following morning as Monday was her day off and decided instead a little gardening was called for.

At the back of her business, she had a patch of concrete where she parked her Land Rover, and beyond that a garden, where she grew a variety of herbs, flowers, vegetables and several fruit trees. But that wasn't where she was heading. Morgana also had a secret garden on her roof where she grew more dangerous plants that she wanted to be sure wouldn't be accidentally eaten by a passing rabbit, or trampled by a child fetching their ball from a neighbouring garden.

She stretched her tired limbs and went up the wooden stairs to the flat she lived in above the shop, and dug around in her kitchen drawer, pulling out her gardening gloves.

The kitchen opened onto a small balcony and from there, she climbed a fire escape up to her private roof terrace.

"Twilight, perfect," Morgana said, looking at the sky and rubbing her hands together with anticipation. She opened a door that looked more like a cupboard, revealing a set of stone steps leading up to her private roof garden. It looked rather bare in midwinter, but she knew the plants had good roots and would flourish again in the spring.

The more dangerous included hemlock, belladonna,

mandrake, datura and henbane, but these weren't what she needed for exorcising a ghost. Instead, she collected some angelica, rosemary, sage and thistle. She would also need onion, garlic and plenty of salt, but those would come from her kitchen. She cut the plants carefully then spent an hour tending to the plot and getting her hands deep in the soil. She knew it was good for her soul to clear her mind and focus on connecting with nature. By the time she was done, her knees were hurting and her back was aching, but she had everything clear in her mind. She'd just washed her hands, ready to call Tristan and discuss the case with him when her phone rang.

Her breath caught as she saw it was Oliver's number. She hadn't realised until that moment how much she had begun to doubt ever hearing from him again.

"Hello?" she answered.

"Morgana, it's Oliver. Is this a good time?"

"Yes, it's perfect. How are you?"

"I've been better. I'm sorry I haven't called, but my sister turned up this week, claiming she's leaving her husband and moving back in with me."

"Goodness. I didn't even know you had a sister."

She could hear the smile in his voice as he replied, "Where do you think Ethan came from?"

Morgana had met Ethan when he'd come to stay with his uncle the same weekend she had been a guest in his house. The whole thing had been very awkward because Ethan had once been in a relationship with Morgana's identical twin sister, Morwenna, and Morgana had been posing as Morwenna at the time.

"One of the Greek statues in your garden came to life and you decided he could be your nephew?" She teased, alluding to the fact that Ethan was rather like a young god in appearance.

"As all my Greek statues have fig leaves with nothing beneath them, I'm not sure Ethan would be too happy with that comparison. However, it might have been for the best; he's currently involved with a young starlet who's spent more time in rehab than out of it, which is yet another thing driving my sister to distraction. So, I just wanted to check in so you didn't think I was being rude by not calling, but the long and short of it is I can't get away at the moment to make another date."

Morgana felt her heart fall into her stomach. Was he making excuses?

"No problem, I'm fairly busy myself and there's lots to do in the shop as I've got to get ready for Yule."

"Good, good. Well, I'll call you when things settle a little here, is that okay?"

"Of course, thanks for letting me know."

She hung up feeling distinctly deflated. Had he merely made the call out of good manners? He was a stickler for such things, but then again, he was also very straight up, so it wasn't like him to fake a story about his sister to avoid something. He was much more likely to just tell her he didn't think it was going to work out between them.

"But how well do you really know him?" she muttered to herself. "Just because he's been honest with you up until now, it doesn't mean he always will be."

Talking to Tristan didn't bring her much joy either.

"Unless you can provide new evidence that Valeria Dawson was murdered, we can't reopen the case."

Tristan said. "You telling me that her ghost told you she didn't pack her clothes or passport just isn't grounds, Morgana. It's not that I don't believe you, and I agree that the husband's statement is very fishy considering what you know, but you've got to bring me actual evidence!"

"And I'm trying to find some," Morgana said, frustrated. "But it's pretty tricky when every person I talk to points me to someone else. I know the time of death though; Valeria heard the clock strike eleven just before she was knocked out, so maybe you could cross-check that against the statements for the night she disappeared, see if anyone doesn't have an alibi for that time?"

"I have a case load on my desk as long as my arm. I'm working, Morgana."

"Stolen bike helmet?" she scoffed, having seen it in the local paper as the crime of the day in Portmage.

"I'm not your 'pet policeman'. Call me if you get something concrete, or better still, call the station." Then he hung up on her.

Morgana took her anger out on her herbs with the use of a pestle and mortar, grinding all the ingredients she needed until they were practically powder. She knew she was supposed to be calm while doing this sort of thing and part of the spell would include projecting the right energies into the mix, but she'd expected a lot more support from Tristan.

"You want proof? I'll keep digging until I get some," she raged as she pummelled and ground the mixture.

She'd intended to take it straight to the bookshop on Monday morning, but instead, she decided to visit Bethany Musgrove first and see if she could get any further along in her investigation.

Armed with the knowledge that the Musgroves' house backed on to Archie Dawson's, Morgana walked to the far end of the village and then down Freezing Lane. The name of the road had always amused her. It faced the sea and was often buffeted by the cold winds that came from the north. She found a long row of squat whitewashed cottages, actually rather pretty despite being designed to weather the English coast rather than for any aesthetic. She guessed that the last in the row was the most likely to back onto Archie's house, and knocked on the door, noting it was named Honeysuckle Cottage. While she waited for an answer, she opened up her senses ready to learn as much as she could from Bethany.

The door opened only a few inches.

"Yes?"

"Mrs. Musgrove? My name's Morgana, I own a shop on the High Street. I was wondering if I could take a few minutes of your time to discuss something?" She kept her voice as gentle as if talking to a child, although she could see that the timid woman in front of her was actually about sixty. Her hair was already white and pulled back into a messy bun, and she wore no make-up. But Morgana could see her aura clearly. She was frightened of strangers, and was radiating a quiet kindness almost at odds with her fear. Morgana already highly doubted that Mrs. Musgrove had it in her to murder anyone, but even the nicest of people could be moved to a violent fit of passion if pushed hard enough.

"I... I think I recognise you. You're one of Delia's daughters?"

"That's right. Can I come in? It's rather cold out here."

Mrs. Musgrove looked nervously over her shoulder, then seemed to check herself and opened the door wider.

"Please do. Your mother and I used to be good friends, you know, when we were younger."

Morgana took note of that, and she could ask her mother later for more information if necessary. "She's still living here in the village," Morgana said. "She owns the art gallery in Lower Portmage."

"I know." Mrs. Musgrove gave a shame-faced nod. "I don't go out anymore. I'm afraid, so I've lost touch with all my old friends. Also, my husband didn't really like me to do things without him, so it's been years since we've talked."

"Is he here?" Morgana asked, remembering Mrs. Musgrove checking behind her. "I can come back at a better time if you'd prefer?" She could hardly discuss Mrs. Musgrove's supposed love for Archie Dawson if her husband was going to be listening.

"No." Mrs. Musgrove gave a small smile. "He's been dead ten years now."

"Oh, then I'm sorry for your loss." Morgana was slightly startled by this news. Ten years? Then he must have died at around the same time that Valeria had. That was certainly suspicious. Perhaps Bethany Musgrove was a serial killer? Or perhaps she'd been in love with Archie Dawson but it was unrequited, so she'd got rid of his wife and her husband hoping they could find comfort together? Morgana thought the theory far-fetched, especially considering how gentle Mrs. Musgrove seemed now, but it was a better reason for Valeria's murder than any other she'd been able to come up with.

"I'm not. He wasn't a very nice man, especially towards the end." Mrs. Musgrove led Morgana past a rather small gloomy looking sitting room, to the back of the house where the kitchen and dining room had been knocked through into one bigger room, and the windows faced south, letting in plenty of winter sunlight. This room was neat and cheerful, painted yellow, with duck egg blue cupboards and wooden worktops.

"Cup of tea?" Mrs. Musgrove filled a kettle at the sink and set it on the gas hob. Morgana was intrigued, she hadn't seen anyone boil a kettle that way since she was a small girl; everyone used electric kettles now.

"Now, before you tell me why you're here, I'd love to hear how your mother is doing?"

Morgana told her all about how her mother had decided to explore her dreams of being a local artist after the death of her father, and how well it was going, and they continued to make small talk until the tea was made.

"Mrs. Musgrove," Morgana began. "The reason I've called around is because I'm investigating the disappearance of Valeria Dawson, on behalf of a mutual friend. I've been talking to various people, and someone mentioned you were friends with the Dawsons around that time, so I was hoping you might be able to shed some light on the circumstances surrounding it."

Mrs. Musgrove's face clouded. "I don't know that I'll be able to help you much. I didn't really know Valeria more than to say hello to. It was Archie I was friends with, I suppose. He was kind to me when I needed it."

Morgana watched emotions flicker through the other

woman's aura and saw some guilt there.

"I take it your husband didn't approve?"

"My husband had been diagnosed with terminal cancer and it made him very bitter. He'd always been a rather angry sort of person, but it got worse." Mrs. Musgrove's hand strayed to her temple and Morgana saw an ugly scar along her hairline.

"He hit you?" she said, softly.

Mrs. Musgrove didn't seem to hear her. "He was bedbound for the last few months, but it didn't stop him lashing out if I got too close. I wasn't allowed to go out and leave him either, or he'd get in a mad rage of jealousy. Archie was the only person I could talk to, as I could speak to him without even leaving the garden. He had his vegetables on one side of the hedge, and I had my flowers on the other. Len couldn't stop me from tending to the flowers as it was the only income we had by then."

Mrs. Musgrove's aura flooded with guilt, and Morgana decided there was something she was hiding.

"What happened?"

"Archie had given me a couple of gifts not long before, and one night, Len saw them and got up from his bed to beat me and said he was going to do the same to Archie. He never made it that far."

"You stopped him?" Morgana pushed, willing Mrs. Musgrove to confess.

"What? No. He collapsed after a few steps and started choking. I called an ambulance and he was moved to an end-of-life ward after that. He only lasted a few more days."

Morgana wondered if perhaps this was why Archie

had decided to get rid of Valeria. Maybe he truly had cared for Bethany Musgrove and now she was free of her husband, he wanted to be free of his wife?

"Was this before Valeria disappeared?" she asked.

But Mrs. Musgrove shook her head. "No, a couple of weeks after."

"Oh." Bang went that theory, though Archie must have known the end was near for Mrs. Musgrove's husband. But it still made more sense the other way around.

She briefly wondered if Mrs. Musgrove's husband might have somehow been involved in Valeria's death. Could he have taken his anger at Archie out on Archie's wife? But that didn't make much sense either. Len might have been violent towards women, but he had nothing to gain by killing Valeria.

"This is a bit awkward to ask, but were you and Archie Dawson romantically involved?"

The guilt washed over Mrs. Musgrove's aura again, but she shook her head. "No."

"Did you want to be?" Morgana couldn't help herself from asking. Jennifer Penwyn had hinted that Mrs. Musgrove had been in love with Archie.

Mrs. Musgrove looked down at her hands, her fingers twisting nervously. "He was very charming. He was interested in things I said and thought; no one else ever has been. He listened and he supported my ideas. It was like a breath of fresh air in my life when I was with him. But we were both married to other people. We were never anything more than friends."

Morgana stared hard at Mrs. Musgrove as she spoke, looking for the tell-tale signs that she was lying, but her aura showed nothing, and Morgana had to conclude that Mrs. Musgrove was telling the truth. They had never been involved, even if they had wanted to be.

"But then his wife vanished and your husband was dying. What was to stop you being together after that?"

Mrs. Musgrove bit a trembling lip. "You wouldn't understand, but when you've spent years under the thumb of a terrible man, you don't trust again so easily. Archie's wife didn't die of natural causes; she was just gone."

Morgana saw the play of emotions in Mrs. Musgrove's aura. Guilt, shame, suspicion.

"You think he did it," Morgana said, speaking without thinking. "You think Archie Dawson killed his wife."

"No, no, of course not!" Mrs. Musgrove looked horrified, but Morgana could see she was lying.

"I'm sorry," Morgana apologised, seeing she'd genuinely upset the other woman. "I'm just trying to piece together every angle. I can see why you wanted to protect yourself from hurt after what you'd been though."

Mrs. Musgrove gave her a forgiving smile, despite the tears in her eyes. "It's funny, but when Len died, I couldn't wait to throw myself back into the land of the living. I wanted to go out every night and be a new person. But it was as though he was haunting me, making sure I could never be free of him. Every time I left the house, something bad seemed to happen to me. I was mugged, then a car tried to run me down. Another time, I was nearly pushed under a bus. I stopped going out after that. My doctor says I'm suffering from a form of PTSD after the years of abuse, and it's made me agoraphobic. I can hardly leave the house anymore."

"But you don't mind having visitors?"

"Who would want to visit me? No-one remembers who I am anymore; I almost don't remember myself now." Her aura became dimmer somehow, as if she'd shrunk even more inside herself and Morgana felt her loneliness like a knife through the heart. So many people seemed lonely in a village that was supposedly all about community.

"How about my mother? I'm sure she'd love to pop in for a cuppa and a chat if you were up to it?"

"She wouldn't. I shunned her, ignored her. I was trying to make Len happy by giving up my friends. It didn't work of course, but by the time I realised it, it was too late. I didn't have any anymore."

"She'll understand. If she wanted to visit you, would you like her to?"

"Yes, I'd like that more than anything." Mrs. Musgrove's tears spilled over and rolled down her cheeks until she fished a tissue out of her pocket and dabbed them away.

"I'm sorry if my questions upset you," Morgana said, feeling like a horrible person.

Mrs. Musgrove flapped a hand at her, continuing to blot her eyes. "No, it's you who should forgive me for being so overemotional. It's been lovely having someone to talk to."

"I'd better be going, but I'll tell my mother I've seen you." Morgana got to her feet and looked out of the kitchen window, down the lawn to where the hedge at the end met Archie Dawson's property.

"Is that Honesty growing over there?"

Mrs. Musgrove bobbed her head in reply.

"If it's not already spoken for, then I'd love to buy some. I don't sell fresh flowers in my shop, but dried Honesty is an extremely popular request for wedding decorations. People often buy stuff like that from me when they want a more Celtic-style wedding. Do you think you might be interested in supplying me with some? I'd give you a good price."

Mrs. Musgrove brightened. "I've got bunches and bunches of it drying in my shed. It's a favourite of mine too."

"Excellent. I'll come back next week if that's okay and we can haggle?"

"I look forward to it."

Morgana left Honeysuckle Cottage, glad that Mrs. Musgrove seemed happier than when she'd arrived. She seemed nothing more than a sweet middle-aged widow, but Morgana knew looks could be deceptive. But her instincts told her that Mrs. Musgrove was no murderer. She did, however, have to agree with Valeria that Mrs. Musgrove also didn't seem like a woman in whom Archie Dawson would be interested. Valeria was strong and attractive and had an attitude that would make a rhino think twice about charging, and then there was Belinda the friendly barmaid who was probably still very attractive to men of a certain age.

Bethany Musgrove was none of those things; she was scared and mousy, exactly as described. Archie had probably just felt sorry for her. Which was nice of him, now she came to think of it.

Morgana felt more confused than ever about a

motive for Valeria's murder, and no further forward in her investigation. Oh well, next on her list was exorcising a ghost!

Chapter Thirteen

Morgana walked slowly to the bookshop, pondering all the way if Bethany Musgrove had given her any useful information.

There were certainly a lot of women in Archie Dawson's life.

Valeria, Maud, Belinda and Mrs. Musgrove. But what about the men in Valeria's life? What had happened to the ex-boyfriend? She'd definitely have to ask about him before she sent Valeria on her way to the next plane.

The bookshop wasn't nearly as full as the last time Morgana had been there, but it was far from empty. Two young children sat at a table looking through picture books while their mother drank a coffee and read something weightier.

An elderly gentleman was browsing the military section, and a girl in her late teens was curled up on the sofa with a lemonade and a bag filled with second-hand books beside her.

"Looks like business is good?" Morgana asked, approaching Rhiannon who was standing behind the counter, a look of serene contentment on her face.

"It really is. I'm incredibly nervous about the newspaper article though. It comes out on Wednesday, and I have no idea what it will say. Would you like to meet for a drink after work that night to either celebrate or commiserate with me?"

"That sounds lovely; I could do with a bit of a girls' night," Morgana agreed.

"Oh dear, man trouble?" Rhiannon laughed, but her eyes were sympathetic.

"A little bit. But nothing a large white wine won't fix."

"It's a date then. Are you here for books or for our ghost?"

"The ghost today." Morgana held up her ghost exorcism bundle. "Valeria said she was ready to cross over, and so hopefully, this should be enough to get her there. As long as the spirit is willing, then it's usually a simple spell."

Rhiannon's face fell slightly. "Oh, I was hoping she might stay around a little longer. I rather like having someone to talk to after hours, and it's kind of like she's looking out for me. Do you know, a teenager tried to walk out of here this morning without paying for a book and Valeria yanked them back as they got to the door and knocked the book out of their hand. Of course, the girl said she had simply forgotten she was holding it, and I gave her the benefit of the doubt, but it was rather nice knowing Valeria was protecting my business."

"Pfff," Valeria commented dismissively, appearing perched on a stack of books. "Tell her to get a dog, I'm not a security guard."

Morgana smiled. "I think you have a heart of gold under that gruff exterior."

"Ugh, whatever. So, you're ready to send me on my way?"

"If you're sure you want to go? We still haven't solved your murder; it could be any day now."

"Or it could be another ten years, or never. Are you any closer to figuring out *who dunnit*?"

"Well, no," Morgana admitted. "There are plenty of suspects, but no real motive so far, and they all seem like nice people."

"Sociopaths can be extremely charming, I've known a couple, really sympathetic and charismatic, but cold as ice underneath," Rhiannon put in, following Morgana's side of the conversation.

"Actually, that sounds more like a *psycho*path. They can fake being kind and understanding, and appear totally normal, maintaining a job and even a relationship. They are generally intelligent and rational but feel no empathy whatsoever. *Socio*paths are usually more hot-headed, and they struggle with fitting into society like keeping up a facade long enough to manage a career or a relationship. They are too impulsive and self-absorbed. But I agree this sounds more like a sociopath, as so far, all the signs point to it being a crime of passion, and sociopaths do flip out and have fits of rage."

"Sounds as though you've done some research," Rhiannon said.

"Solving murders has become a bit of a side hobby for me, especially since I can sometimes use my abilities to help the police, so I may have done a tiny bit of reading on the subject," Morgana said, feeling a bit embarrassed to know so much about the mentality of killers. "On the other hand, there could be a rational explanation for the murder, like money. You don't have to be psychotic to cross that line when a lot of money is involved."

"I think anyone who murders another person is mentally unbalanced."

"Yes, I agree. I just meant it can take a lot of different forms, and it may be that someone felt they had no choice."

"No one had a gun to their head when it came to me," Valeria said. "You said yourself, there's no obvious motive so far."

"No, the only ones I can find seem to revolve around your husband and all the women who liked him. Which brings me to something I meant to ask you about; is there any chance at all that it might have been a man in your life rather than a woman in his?"

"What man? The delivery driver on the truck? He was married with six kids but probably the only person I actually spent any time talking to." Valeria's sarcasm was sharp.

"I meant the ex-boyfriend Archie said you kept in touch with."

"Oh, Clarke." Valeria had the grace to look shamefaced. "I didn't know Archie knew about that. Clarke was a fantasy more than anything. We were together at school and stayed in touch even when he moved away to Singapore for a job. He was very *jet set,* while Archie was very down to earth. I suppose I was attracted to the glamour and the idea of him, but in reality, it was never really me."

"And he still liked you too?"

"He said he never found the right woman after me, and maybe he was telling the truth because he never married. But to be honest, I don't think he was the marrying type; he enjoyed being a playboy too much to settle."

"So, you never saw each other in the months leading up to your disappearance? And he had no reason to come and kill you?" Morgana slumped as yet another potential lead looked like being a dead end.

"Of course not. In fact, I actually told him to stop emailing me a few days before, well, you know." Valeria mimed being bashed on the head.

"Why did you tell him to stop if you'd kept in touch all those years?"

"He was due to come back to the UK for a conference and invited me to visit him in his hotel in London. That was a little too close to home for me, so I decided the fantasy had run its course."

"Maybe that was his motive?" Morgana said, perking up. "Maybe he was serious about being in love with you and actually thought you'd leave your husband one day, until you told him otherwise?"

Valeria shook her head. "Hardly likely. He's not going to come all the way here to get me back then decide to kill me without even attempting to persuade me first, is he?"

"I suppose not."

"So, are we going to do this crossing over thing or not?" Valeria tapped a foot impatiently.

Morgana waited for Rhiannon to serve a customer and then asked if they could use the basement.

"Sure, I can't leave the shop floor, but let me know how it goes. And Valeria, if you can hear me, thanks for being a good sport."

"Yeah, no sweat." Valeria looked secretly gratified.

Morgana spent some time cleansing the basement area with a sage smudge stick, hoping she wouldn't set off any smoke alarms as there was no ventilation down there.

"At least it smells better than it did," Valeria commented.

"Yes, all the underground cave-type basements I've been in have been rather dank, but this one has a real sense of disuse and neglect," Morgana agreed. "Now, I want you to stand in the middle of the room and I'm going to pour a circle of salt around you, okay?"

"So, it's true evil spirits can't cross salt?" Valeria looked on with interest as Morgana began to walk a slow circle around her, making sure there was no gap in the line. "What about *nice* spirits like me?"

"It works for all spirits, most demons too. But this isn't just to contain you, I'm also making a sacred circle to gather energy into."

"You can do that with salt?"

"You can do it with anything actually, even a marker pen would be fine. Salt is traditional though. The difference is me, not the salt. I'm imbuing my magic into it as I go, and then for the final touch to close it…" Morgana took a knife out of her bundle.

It was her athame, a knife she kept cleansed of negative energy and that she had soaked overnight in water gathered during a waning moon, to mark the ending of a passage.

She raised the knife and then stabbed it quickly into her own palm. She clenched her fist with a slight hiss of pain as the blood welled up under the cut, and then held her closed fist over the salt, squeezing it tight until a few drops of blood trickled out and landed in the salt. There was a small crackle of energy and Valeria flinched.

"I felt that." Valeria reached out her hands towards the salt and came into contact with an invisible wall. "How far up does this go?"

"All the way," Morgana said. "All the way up and all

the way down, a distance more than we can measure."

"Huh, so I guess there's nowhere to go but up or down."

"I don't think it works like that; it's another plane of existence. You'll just vanish."

"Been there, done that, worn out the t-shirt."

Morgana laughed at Valeria's quip and then began to circle her, keeping outside the line of salt. As she circled, she said a simple chant.

Spirits from the other side
I call upon you to guide
Valeria Dawson to where she should be
This is my will, so mote it be.

As she finished repeating the spell for the third time, Morgana pulled out a pouch where she'd stored the powder she'd created with her herbs and cast a handful of the contents into the circle.

For a moment, she thought it was working as Valeria began to dematerialise, but then Valeria let out a shriek and clutched at her neck.

The golden scarf around it seemed to be yanking her backwards.

"*This is my will,*" Morgana said, more forcefully, throwing another handful of powder of Valeria.

Once again, she seemed to be leaving, only to be yanked back again. Valeria clutched at her throat, spluttering against the pressure of the scarf, and trying to pull it away from her neck.

"This bloody awful thing seems to be tied to something here, and why can't I get it off?"

Morgana shrugged. "I'm sorry, I have no idea."

"Do I really have to spend the rest of eternity in this hideous thing? It's so not me!" Valeria kept running a finger around the inside of scarf, trying to loosen it.

"Actually, I have a theory. You said before you didn't remember wearing the scarf the night you died, right?"

"I wouldn't be seen dead in this colour. Well, apart from the fact that I am being seen dead in it."

"Right, so let's assume you weren't wearing it that night. But now you are, and it seems to be keeping you from moving on," Morgana said, circling Valeria again, but this time deep in thought.

"Potato tomato, what are you getting at?"

"Your killer put it around your neck."

Valeria's eyes widened as she considered that. "Yeah, makes sense, but why? And why is it so bloody tight?"

"I think you were strangled with it. Which means…" Morgana paused to kick a gap in the circle of salt and free Valeria. "Which means you are definitely stuck here until we figure this out, and not only that, I think also, the scarf may be a key to the mystery."

Chapter Fourteen

Morgana was looking forward to her night out with Rhiannon, especially as it was to be a celebration rather than a commiseration. The article on the bookshop had come out in the local paper and it was glowing. There was even a photo of a book hovering in mid-air, albeit slightly blurry, but enough to pique some people's interest.

"It was a dark and stormy night," Morgana said, as she made her way down the High Street from her shop to Rhiannon's. It was at times like these that Morgana was glad she was so familiar with every nook and cranny of the village. Shapes loomed in the darkness and she felt strangely on edge. The sea was crashing noisily against the cliffs below, and she could taste the salt spray in the air. The pub would be warm and welcoming though, and she was eager to collect her new friend and get inside. They might even get a table by the log fire as it was a weeknight and low season for tourists.

She stopped in confusion when she reached the bookshop. Rhiannon had definitely told her to meet her there, but the place was in darkness.

Maybe Rhiannon had decided to go home and change first and was on her way back? Morgana pulled her coat more tightly around herself and leaned against the door, stumbling as it opened. She took an unsteady step backwards, finding herself inside the bookshop.

Why hadn't Rhiannon closed the door properly? Had she left in a rush?

Morgana froze as a bump in the night sounded, seeming to come from inside rather than out.

"Rhiannon?" Morgana called out. She knew there was a bank of light switches to the left of the door and she fumbled her way over to them. Flicking the switches did nothing.

Either a fuse had blown or the main switch had been tripped.

If Rhiannon's building was anything like hers, then the main fuse box would be at the back where the electricity lines came in, but Morgana had no idea exactly where.

"Rhiannon, are you back here?"

Morgana took a few steps and bumped into a chair. If her friend was sorting out the lights, then wouldn't she still be near enough to answer?

Morgana quickly took down the walls in her mind and reached out with her senses. She wasn't alone in the building, and was getting conflicting emotions coming at her. Anger and fear predominantly.

"Valeria? I need you," Morgana whispered, but there was no response.

Fumbling in her handbag, Morgana pulled out her phone and shook it, creating a beam of torchlight. It was a bit thin, but better than nothing. That was when she heard what sounded like a choked scream coming from below her.

The edgy feeling intensified and she decided against calling out again. It was possible Rhiannon had simply fallen in the darkness, but her senses told her that wasn't the case.

Morgana swung her phone around finding the door to the basement and rushed towards it.

It was pitch black and she cursed silently as her light

picked out only a thin beam directly in front of her. She was going to do nothing but give away her own position, and she'd only see something if her phone was directly pointing at it.

She paused, shook her phone again so the light went out, and closed her eyes. She needed to be able to see what was happening without light, and the only way she could think of to do that would be to open her third eye.

Doing so would make her blind to the real world, but that was irrelevant in the absolute darkness of the basement. It would also disorientate her and leave her too exhausted to move, but not immediately. She'd get a little time before it became overpowering, and her friend might need her help *now*.

It seemed to take several very long seconds as she shifted the world from normal sight to her third eye. It was a bit like seeing a photo negative, and everything would be grey. Everything but a living being. Living beings would be a technicolour of emotions. She would see the colours of their souls.

She opened her eyes, even though she wasn't really using them anymore and saw the outline of the steps going down in front of her. She took them slowly, being as quiet as she could until the room below came into view.

Two figures immediately glowed across the room. One lying on its back, clawing at the other. The second was sitting on the chest of the first and pulling at something wound around the neck of the first.

She was sure the woman lying on the floor was Rhiannon, her soul radiating a bright and colourful life force. But even as Morgana registered what she was seeing, that vibrant life force was dimming. The second figure was a pulsing mass of dark red. Morgana gasped; she'd seen that colour before and knew without a doubt she was looking at a murderer. The anger was soul deep, and left no room for anything else to show through.

Without thinking, she rushed the two figures. "Stop!"

The dark red figure rose to its feet like a devil turning towards her, but they were just as blind in the darkness as she had been and ran headlong into her. Morgana was knocked back and fell awkwardly over a box of books, allowing the other to make their escape. She heard them pounding up the stairs and across the floor above, but she didn't care. Her only thought was to get to Rhiannon. Her friend's life force was weak now, barely showing at all, and losing light every second. She crawled quickly over and began to frantically pull at whatever was around Rhiannon's neck. She could feel it was one of Rhiannon's scarves by the smooth texture, but it was so tight, and there was no sound of Rhiannon drawing breath.

"Come on, breathe Rhiannon." She just hoped her windpipe wasn't completely crushed.

Morgana fumbled for her handbag still looped around her shoulder and pulled her phone out again, punching 999 and asking for an ambulance.

She ignored the requests for information, gave the address and then started CPR. She had no idea if it would do any good at all, but she had to do something. She could still see Rhiannon was alive by the flicker of white light coming from her heart, but it should have been suffusing her entire body if she was alive and well, and instead it was so small, as though her friend was hanging on by a thread.

"Please, please, be okay," she said, pushing hard on her rib cage and hoping she wasn't doing more damage than good. She kept blowing air into her lungs and pushing, with no awareness of time. She only knew it felt like forever. Her brain had already figured out that an ambulance would take at least fifteen minutes to get there, a massive downside to living in a seaside village. She debated stopping and calling the lifeguards; they were closer and they'd know almost as much as a paramedic, but she didn't want to risk it.

The exhaustion began to sweep over her. As if keeping up CPR wasn't exhausting enough on its own, the fact she'd opened her third eye was draining all the remaining energy she had. Any moment now, she knew she was going to collapse into a faint, but she had to keep going. She had to.

Footsteps sounded above and her heart thudded loudly in her ears. Was the killer back to finish the job? She didn't have the energy to fight them off.

She heard them coming down the stairs, they had a powerful torch, but she hardly saw the light. Instead, she saw the soul—a male soul—all black but covered in pinpricks of white, like stars on the darkest night. On his head there blazed a crown of purest light. There only one person she'd ever know with that soul.

"Tristan," she gasped, dropping to her hands and knees with relief.

"Morgana? Are you hurt?"

"Not me. It's Rhiannon, she's not breathing, I can't keep…" Words failed her as she slumped face first into the dust beside her friend.

"I've got it." Tristan instantly took over the CPR, giving the movements more weight and more breath than Morgana had been able to manage in her weakened state.

Morgana just lay there, unable to move or help. Instead, she focussed her mind on shutting down her third eye. She wanted to keep it open to check on Rhiannon's life force, but she'd only exhaust herself more by prolonging its use. She wouldn't need it now; she was safe. She was with Tristan.

Once her third eye was closed, Morgana still couldn't see a thing. She knew there was a torch on, but she was blind. Experience had taught her she'd remain that way for at least half an hour after using her third eye.

Was it her imagination, or had Rhiannon drawn a breath on her own?

Morgana pushed herself up on her hands, straining to hear. Yes, definitely a rasping breath coming from beside her. Morgana at last allowed herself to fall into a faint, and the last thing she heard as she lost consciousness was the sound of sirens.

Chapter Fifteen

Morgana came to slowly, aware she was sitting on a hard floor, a blanket wrapped around her, and a warm body at her back. Everything was still dark.

"Is it dark or is it my eyes?" she asked.

Tristan tightened his arms around her. "It's dark, but we have a torch. I was going to go and look for the fuse box but didn't want to leave you."

"Rhiannon?" she asked.

"I think she's going to be alright. The paramedics say her throat is very bruised but hopefully no permanent damage, and she was unconscious. It looks as though she was knocked out by a blow to the head, but she must have come around at some point because there are signs of a struggle down here. There's a lamp over there that I'm guessing was kicked over, the bulb is smashed. I've called the station and PC Dunn is on her way over to process the scene. We'll have a better idea of what happened after that. We'll need you to give a statement too, but not now, just sit here and rest. I can't find any sign of injury on you, so I'm assuming you're suffering from psychic pain rather than physical?"

Morgana smiled. "That's what makes it so easy being around you. You understand all the psychic stuff without me having to explain."

"Pet policemen have their uses."

Morgana closed her tired eyes, leaning into him.

Tristan was so much more than a pet policeman to her.

They'd grown up in the same village as children, which was why he knew all about her family and had always simply accepted there were witches among them. He might have learned to doubt it as an adult, just as many did, but instead, he had been in a relationship as a teenager with Morgana's twin sister, Morwenna, who had never hidden her powers from him. Morwenna could move energy around, and there was no denying it was real.

Morgana knew she'd had feelings of her own for Tristan; he'd been three years above them at school and her first serious crush. But she'd put them aside after he'd got together with her sister. That was just as big a no-go zone as it was possible to get.

The fact it had been nearly fifteen years ago, and they'd been just teenagers at the time, didn't change anything as far as Morgana was concerned.

But it didn't help that he was still gorgeous and still made her heart flutter.

"I tried to tell Oliver about my powers," she confessed. "But I'm not sure he believed me."

"This is the Lord of the Manor new boyfriend, I take it?"

"Yes. But he might think I'm crazy now and not want to be involved anymore."

Tristan was silent for a long moment and Morgana began to think he wasn't going to say anything when he gave a sigh. "He probably just needs time to adjust. It can be quite intimidating knowing you can see how we feel."

"I kept my senses shut down as much as possible. I've already seen enough to know he's an honest man."

"So you've finally found your King Arthur?"

Morgana shrugged. "I feel he could be."

"Then I'm sure it will work out. Don't hide what you are, Morgana. He'll see what you can do and how much you use it to help people. You saved Miss Lebeau's life tonight."

"Thanks Tristan, you're a good friend."

"I know. Now, do you feel ready to answer some questions? I don't suppose you saw who attacked Miss Lebeau, did you?"

"No. I just saw their soul. I couldn't even tell you if it was a man or a woman. But they were so very, very angry, and there was madness too, a deep-rooted sickness."

"Anything else that can help us?"

Morgana told him about the lights being off and the sounds she'd heard, but knew none of it would really lead him to whoever it was. "I don't even know if they were wearing gloves or anything," she finished. "But I guess you'll check for fingerprints. I'm just hugely relieved you got here so fast. Hey, how did you do that?"

"Poppy was at the station when the call came in, and she immediately rang me because she knew I was in Portmage tonight, having dinner with my mum and brother."

"Are you often in Portmage? I never see you."

"I'm here about twice a week. I live in Wadebridge though. I have a nice place actually; no sea view of course, but pretty good for a Detective Sergeant's salary. You should come by some time." He checked himself. "Or perhaps not. Might be a bit too intimate, especially as we've decided to just be friends. I retract my invitation."

Morgana gave a low chuckle. "You say the most

romantic things, especially in a dark smelly cellar."

Tristan sniffed the air. "It is rather smelly, isn't it. Actually, it smells really putrid and seems to be getting worse."

"I was just thinking that. My eyesight is beginning to come back and I'd really like to get out of here. I feel a bit sick."

Tristan got to his feet. "Hang on just a moment, I need to check something." He picked up his torch from where he'd propped it on a box and began to look around. "It's coming from the back wall, I think." He took a few steps. "Whoa!"

"What? What is it?"

"There's a hole in the ground, wait, no, it's a trap door. It goes down to yet another level below. It must have been hidden in the dirt and dust."

"Tristan, I have a bad feeling, don't go down there."

"I have to Morgana, and I'm pretty sure I know what that smell is."

"Me too," she mumbled, pulling the blanket over her nose and mouth. The smell reminded her of a tomb; there was a very decomposed body close by.

Chapter Sixteen

It was less than ten minutes later that PC Poppy Dunn arrived on the scene and got the lights working again.

Morgana thought it was almost even more grizzly to be able to see the trap door, than when she'd been aware of it but unable to see it in the dark.

The single bare bulb in the cellar illuminated the hole and made shadows of boxes move around the walls as it swung in a breeze created by the open shop door above.

"Ugh, it feels like it's haunted or something down here," Poppy commented, her nose wrinkling at the smell.

Morgana looked around, realising how strange it was that Valeria hadn't made any kind of appearance. She also noticed the trapdoor was exactly where Rhiannon had originally placed the boxes and Valeria had pushed them down. Had Valeria known about the trapdoor marking her grave, or had she been acting on instinct, trying to show them where it was without even knowing why?

"Valeria?" Morgana hissed as quietly as she could, seating herself on the steps away from the action.

"Is it gone?" Valeria's head popped through the wall.

"Is what gone?"

"The evil. There was evil here again."

"Yes, it's gone for now. We've found your body, Valeria, or at least we assume it's you but we won't know for sure until a post-mortem is done. But whoever was here tonight tried to kill Rhiannon and it's clearly the same person who killed you."

"Is Rhiannon okay? I don't want anything to happen to her."

Morgana was touched by the concerned expression on Valeria's face. She acted hard as nails but clearly, she'd become fond of the new proprietor.

"She's bruised and battered, but she should be fine."

"Good. How do you know it was the same person who killed me? It's been ten years."

"Because they knew about the trapdoor over there. It was opened. I think they intended to kill Rhiannon and drop her down there, which is exactly where your body was. I just can't believe you were there beneath our feet all that time, I was sure you were killed here, but I never considered you might be buried here too."

"My body is going to look disgusting." Valeria gave a shudder.

"It's going to be nothing but bones by now, I should think. But that level below was almost airtight and the smell is pretty grim. Did you never realise it was there?"

"No. I had no idea there was another room below this one. Though it's not that odd really, the whole cliff is riddled with caves made by streams over the millennia. Archie may have known it was there; it could have been in the deeds or something I suppose, but I never even noticed it when I used to come down here."

"Yet you blew all the boxes off the entrance to it when Rhiannon covered it," Morgana pointed out.

"I don't know why I did that. I just knew they bothered me."

"I guess that makes sense. And you could feel the presence of your killer. That could be helpful."

"Yeah, it's a horrible feeling, same as the other

night."

Morgana's eyes widened as she comprehended what Valeria was saying. Her killer had been at the bookshop opening.

The next morning, Morgana was awoken by the telephone ringing.

"Hello?" she answered sleepily.

"It's Tristan. I just wanted to update you."

"You have news?" Morgana sat up in bed, disturbing her cat, Lancelot, who removed himself from the bedspread with an angry flick of his tail.

"Yes. We've confirmed the corpse *was* that of Valeria Dawson, and we're on our way now to arrest Archie Dawson. I know I asked you to bring me proof, and you've succeeded, it's no longer a missing persons case, it's now officially a murder investigation."

After hanging up the phone with Tristan, Morgana lay back on her pillows to think over what she knew. It made sense to arrest Archie.

He'd had motive, though only so far as their marriage hadn't been perfect.

He'd also lied about Valeria packing a suitcase to leave him, and he potentially had another woman, though Morgana hadn't worked out yet which one it might be.

He also had no alibi for the night Valeria disappeared, and he'd been at the bookshop opening party when Valeria had possibly sensed her killer among the crowd.

If she had, then it did explain why Valeria had felt pushed out by evil that night and again the night the same person returned to do the same to Rhiannon.

But why would Archie want to hurt Rhiannon?

Why lease her the premises if he just intended to kill her? Unless he was a serial killer of course, who simply murdered without motive. Was that possible?

There were still a lot of questions in her mind, but hopefully, Archie may be able to provide some answers. Tristan had finished the call with her by saying that if she wasn't too exhausted, would she like to be present at his interview and see if she could add any insight to his interrogation?

She definitely wanted to. She felt involved and owed it to Valeria to help her find peace. Valeria was stuck until her murder was solved.

Morgana showered, dressed and fed Lancelot, before grabbing some tea and toast and making her way to her car.

She'd left a note on the door of her shop saying she was closed for the day; some things were more important than being open for a few straggling tourists in the depths of winter.

It was about a thirty-minute drive to the police station and she mulled over the case some more as she went. Bethany Musgrove hadn't been at the bookshop opening, so it ruled her out, assuming Morgana's theory was correct about Valeria sensing her killer's presence.

But Archie Dawson had been there, and Valeria had disappeared almost exactly as he'd arrived. Which made him look even more guilty. Was there a motive she was missing?

Belinda had been at the bookshop that night too.

Maybe even Maud had been there?

It had been crowded enough that Morgana could have missed seeing her. It could have been any of them. And what about Valeria's ex-boyfriend, Morgana wouldn't recognise him, and the only person who could was Valeria, who'd been driven away. She'd have to get Tristan to look into whether he was still in England or had recently returned.

The police could check things like that, couldn't they?

She pulled into a parking space and went inside, finding PC Cartwright manning the front desk with his usual dour demeanour. She'd worked with him before, but if he ever recognised her, then he gave no sign of it.

"Yes?"

"Can you let DS Treharne know Morgana Emrys is here to see him?"

"Fine." He seemed to huff at the effort of picking up a phone and Morgana decided to take a seat rather than linger at the desk being glared at.

Tristan wasn't long. "Morgana, thanks for coming. Are you happy sitting in on the actual interview? That way, you can ask questions as soon as you see a lie."

"Um, sure. But won't DI Lowen disapprove of that? Doesn't he normally take the lead in murder cases?"

"Yes, but he's on holiday at the moment, so I'm afraid it's down to us. He's much more experienced than I am, so I need all the help I can get. Archie Dawson just seems like a nice man, like someone's dad, so it's actually uncomfortable putting the thumbscrews on him, metaphorically of course."

"Does that mean you want me to play bad cop?"

Tristan laughed, and showed her to the interview

room. Together, they peered through tinted window at Archie sitting inside, twisting his hands together nervously.

"Ready?" Tristan asked.

"Wait, I'm sure after ten years it's impossible to establish a time of death," Morgana said. "But Valeria told me the church bells had rung 11pm just a minute or so before she was knocked out. So, we do actually know when the killer arrived. Are we allowed to use that as time of death to get alibis?"

Tristan looked thoughtful.

"I'm not sure it will hold up in court unless we get a confession, but as the post-mortem hasn't even come back yet, I don't see why we can't work to that premise."

"Good. Also, I'm pretty sure she was strangled with a gold satin scarf. Her ghost is wearing one and she complained it was too tight, as well as saying she'd never have chosen to wear it. Archie has a box of gold satin scarves in his hallway."

"Hmm, well, we can use it to suggest means, especially if they belong to him, but if there's a whole box of them, then couldn't he have given one to anybody?"

"Yes." Morgana grimaced. "He did give them away fairly freely to various women over the years, but we can discount anyone who got one after the murder. Also, we can discount anyone who still has one, because they will have used theirs to murder Valeria."

"I'll have Poppy start chasing that up straight away. Anything else you can think of? I'm assuming you don't want to open your third eye again and take a look at his inner self?"

"You assume correct. Once in a week is more than enough; I just couldn't, it's too draining."

"No problem." Tristan put a hand on her back. "Shall we go in?" He opened the door to the interview room.

The first thing Morgana noticed, now she could see him properly, was how pale Mr. Dawson still looked. Guilty complex or just stunned about them finding his wife's body after all this time and confirming she really was dead?

He'd seemed to believe Morgana when she'd told him about Valeria's ghost, but nothing drove it home like uncovering her corpse in the building he owned.

"Mr. Dawson, I'm DS Treharne, and this is Morgana Emrys, a police consultant."

"We've met," Archie said, giving Morgana a confused look.

"Has PC Dunn informed you of why you're here?"

"Someone attacked Ms Lebeau, and for some reason, you think it's me. I can't imagine why; she's renting a property from me, nothing more."

"We have reason to believe the attack was perpetrated by the same person who murdered your wife. They revealed the location of her body. So we'd like to discuss both her murder and the attempted murder of Rhiannon Lebeau. Starting with where you were at 6.30pm last night."

"You've found Valeria's body? Where?"

"In your premises, Mr. Dawson. In a second cellar no one knew about, except perhaps the owner of the property?"

Morgana sat and watched all the emotions he was

feeling flicker through his aura. He was scared, which was understandable, and yet somehow relived. Was that because he wanted to be caught and punished? She knew some people felt that way, as though they couldn't help themselves from doing what they did.

"It's a relief, you know," Archie said, as though reading her mind. "I always assumed she was dead, but knowing for sure, well, it means I can move on properly."

"You'll be moving on to a prison cell unless you can tell me where you were last night," Tristan persisted.

Archie spread his hands. "Home, alone. I can tell you what I was watching on TV if that would help?"

"It doesn't." Tristan leaned forward. "According to your previous statement regarding your wife, you were also home alone that night too."

"That's where I am most of the time."

"And do you happen to remember what you were watching at 11pm on the night she went missing?" Tristan asked, looking sceptical.

"11pm? Are you sure?" Archie's eyes widened, and Morgana saw a flush of guilt wash over him.

She leaned forward. "Does that time mean something to you, Mr. Dawson? It looked as though you remembered something."

"I…" He faltered, "no."

Tristan shot a look at Morgana, then back at Archie. "It won't help you to hide anything. We'll be going into that night a lot more deeply this time, talking again to everyone who might have been involved. All your friends and neighbours. It would save them a lot of trouble if you just told us."

Archie twisted his hands again, and his voice came out almost a whisper. "I… I wasn't alone at 11pm. One of my neighbours was having an argument with her husband that night. He was violent towards her; domestic abuse I think you call it. I saw her run out of the house into the garden and I went out to check she was alright. That was at 11pm. We talked for a while, and then she went back into her house and I went back to mine and went to bed. What's really awful is that I remember being glad at that point that Valeria hadn't come home yet. She could be jealous."

Morgana gave Tristan a nod to confirm she could see he was speaking the truth.

"The name of the neighbour, please." Tristan's pen hovered over his note pad. "We'll have to verify this."

"I'd rather not say." Archie folded his arms.

"Bethany Musgrove," Morgana supplied.

Archie looked startled. "Please don't speak to her. She's been through so much already. She's not strong enough to be questioned like this."

"She's your alibi for your wife's murder," Tristan said. "Would you rather go to prison than have her confirm your statement?"

Morgana reached out to pat Mr. Dawson's hand. "She will be glad to know it wasn't you. She cares a great deal for you, but she's terrified you were the one who murdered Valeria, so it will be a huge relief for her."

"Nothing happened between us," Archie blurted out. "We were only talking. But she hasn't spoken to me since I made a stupid mistake. I told her I loved her and I thought it scared her away. She's so good and sweet. Did she really think it was me? Is that why she's avoided me ever since?"

"I suppose the fact you told her you loved her and then your wife conveniently vanished may have spooked her a little," Morgana said.

"Even if your alibi checks out, we still need to find out if there is any connection between you and the attack on Ms Lebeau," Tristan said. "And let's discuss the fact you said your wife packed her bags and took her passport, which clearly she can't have done as she never left the shop on the High Street."

"I knew it was a stupid thing to say as soon as I'd said it. I panicked. Bethany was avoiding me and people were whispering I'd done away with Val. I thought if there was evidence she'd gone away, then it would stop. It didn't, of course."

"Mr. Dawson, is there any chance you can remember everyone you gave one of your golden scarves to? Before Valeria was murdered, that is," Morgana asked, ignoring Tristan's warning look.

"Um, my sister's daughters, my nieces. They were only about eleven and twelve at the time though. I did also give one to Bethany and a couple of other people. I'd have to think about it; it was a long time ago. Is it relevant?"

"Yes, I want a list," Tristan said.

"I'll do my best. But you can rule Bethany out now, can't you? After all, she was with me at the time of the murder."

"Unless you were in on it together. We are going to keep you a while longer while we check your alibi." Tristan folded his notebook shut, indicating the interview was over for now.

"I told you the scarf was a major clue," Morgana said as soon as they were alone in Tristan's office. "We need to find someone who was given one but doesn't have it anymore. Whoever it was, they used it to strangle Valeria."

"They could have taken it away again afterwards?" Tristan said.

Morgana shook her head. "I don't think so, Valeria's wearing it. I think they left it on her."

"Forensic evidence will confirm if that's the case."

"So, what's our next move?"

"I need to ask Bethany Musgrove to come in for questioning. But it sounds like it's going to be a dead end, because if they can alibi each other, then we're back to square one."

"You can't ask Mrs. Musgrove to come in, it would be cruel. She's agoraphobic. Much better if we go and visit her."

"We?" Tristan raised his eyebrows.

"Yes, she's scared of her own shadow. You need me there to soften it a bit. But then what? Have you looked into the ex-boyfriend angle?"

"Actually, that's my next line of enquiry. After your last call, I began to go back over the file and read all the emails between him and Valeria. She'd just cut contact between them and he was none too happy about it, and funnily enough, he was in the UK at the time of her disappearance."

"We're finally making progress; he's got to be the bad guy."

Morgana was delighted with this news. She hadn't really wanted Mr. Dawson or Mrs. Musgrove to be guilty. But some faceless boyfriend from Valeria's past was perfect as the shadowy murderer. "Except for one detail," she said with a grimace. "What possible motive could he have for trying to kill Rhiannon?"

Chapter Seventeen

Tristan and Morgana took separate cars back to Portmage, and then met up at the end of Freezing Lane.

"You'll need to be very gentle with her, and let me do most of the talking," Morgana said. "I don't think she feels much at ease around men after what she went through with her husband."

"But you think she likes Mr. Dawson?"

"Yes, but he's a very non-threatening man, isn't he? His manner is always gentle and charming, so I can see why he brings her out of herself. You, on the other hand, are rather more masculine and project an aura saying you're the one in control. It'll make her nervous."

"I do?" Tristan looked pleased.

Morgana tutted at him and rang the bell. When the door opened a crack as before, she positioned herself so she was blocking Tristan from view.

"Mrs. Musgrove, it's me again, Morgana. I have a police detective with me who wants to ask you a few questions, may we come in?"

Mrs. Musgrove opened the door wider, and Morgana could instantly see she'd been crying. "Yes, please do."

She didn't go into the bright sunny kitchen this time, but instead led them into the gloomy sitting room, where she sank onto an armchair, a box of tissues at her side. Morgana and Tristan seated themselves on the sofa diagonally opposite her in the small room.

"I'm sorry, I should have lit the fire," Mrs. Musgrove sniffled. "But I didn't have the heart. I saw Archie being taken away earlier from my bedroom window. So, he did do it?"

"Did do what, Mrs. Musgrove?" Tristan said, clearly not wanting to immediately tip his hand.

"He murdered Valeria. I was afraid he had, and it's all my fault. I told him if he was free, then things would be different, but he wasn't and that was that. Then she was gone, and it's like I wished it on her." She dabbed at her eyes as more tears fell.

"You know why we're here?" Tristan said.

She nodded. "The postman told me Valeria's body was found last night."

"Can I ask why you didn't tell us you'd seen Mr. Dawson on the night she disappeared?"

"When the police first questioned me ten years ago, my husband was still alive. I wanted to be honest, but couldn't risk it. He would have killed me, you see. He was so suspicious and so very volatile; even at that stage, he had the power left in him to exact revenge if he was angry enough. But I suppose that doesn't matter now."

Morgana's eyes widened as a new idea hit her. "Do you think he could have gone to the shop where she worked looking for Mr. Dawson, but then Valeria got in his way?"

But Mrs. Musgrove shook her head. "He was too sick, couldn't even get down the stairs. When he was taken to the end-of-life hospice only a few days later, they had to carry him out on a stretcher."

"We understand you did in fact see Mr. Dawson on the night his wife disappeared, and I was wondering if you could confirm what time that was and how long you were talking?"

"It was almost exactly eleven. I heard the church bells when I went into the garden. We talked for about half an hour. Is it relevant?"

"Yes, Mrs. Musgrove, it's extremely relevant." Tristan was already putting his notebook away with reluctance. "We now know Mrs. Dawson was murdered a few minutes after eleven, which means Archie Dawson is completely innocent."

Bethany Musgrove stared at them as though she couldn't quite comprehend what Tristan was saying.

"He's innocent?"

"His story matches yours, yes. Which means he was with you at the time of the murder."

"All these years," Mrs. Musgrove said, staring at the wall, "all these years, I've shunned him and ignored him, and it wasn't him. I didn't even give him a chance to tell me."

"I don't think he holds it against you," Morgana said, softly. "He understood your fear."

"He's a wonderful man, and I've wronged him."

Mrs. Musgrove began to cry even harder, and Tristan looked awkward.

"I think we had best be on our way. Thank you so much for your time; you've been very helpful."

"Just one more question." Morgana held up her hand to halt him. "Did Archie give you a gold scarf, and do you still have it if so?"

"He did, but I was mugged. Do you remember me saying? The mugger took it."

"They took the scarf? Anything else?" Tristan was instantly alert.

"No, just the scarf, it was pulled off my neck so hard I spun around and fell. They ran off after that."

"Can you remember anything about the mugger?

Did you file a report?"

"No, I didn't report it, it was just a scarf, and it was dark, so I didn't see anything. It was just one thing in a long list of bad things that seemed to be happening to me at the time, so it seemed safer just to stay inside after that."

Tristan and Morgana walked slowly back down the lane. "Well, Mr. Dawson's alibi checks out," Tristan said. "I'm very glad for him he has one. You know how I feel about the wrong person going to prison."

"I do. You'd rather the murderer went free than arrest the wrong man. I like that about you," Morgana said. "But you have to agree the scarf is significant. The only problem is the list of who Archie gave a scarf to is useless now, because if I'm right, then the killer still has one."

"What do you mean?" Tristan said.

"Mrs. Musgrove was mugged for her scarf not long after Valeria was killed. The killer used theirs on Valeria and then took Mrs. Musgrove's. Which makes me think the murderer is a woman. A man wouldn't wear a scarf like that; it's too feminine."

"I think you're right," Tristan agreed. "But it could be deliberate misdirection. The box of scarves is in Mr. Dawson's hallway, so almost anyone calling at the house could have stolen one."

"Then why take Mrs. Musgrove's? It seems personal to have targeted her. She told me someone had tried to push her under a bus, and a car almost ran her down. I think staying inside all these years may have saved her life. I think the murderer wanted to murder her too."

"That makes it rather unlikely to have been Valeria's

ex-boyfriend then, as he had no motive for hurting Mrs. Musgrove or Rhiannon either. Which means we're out of suspects."

"Yes." Morgana stared at the sea. "No suspects, no leads, except one."

She knew Tristan thought she meant the ex-boyfriend, but she had a completely different idea. In fact, thinking about it, she had two people yet to be exonerated and it was time she stepped up the stakes.

Chapter Eighteen

As Morgana let herself into the shop, with no regrets about the day of lost business, her phone began to ring. Her heart jumped as she saw it was Oliver, and a smile crossed her face even though she also felt a flutter of nerves.

It had to be a good sign he was calling again so soon?

"Oliver," she said, trying to sound composed.

"Hello, Morgana. Is it a good time?" She noticed he was always considerate enough to check.

"Yes, it is. How are you?"

"Slightly frazzled. My sister is driving me potty. Her husband's turned up and they've been having a high old time hurling my antiques at each other all day. It's easy to see where Ethan gets his flair for the dramatic. The whole thing seems to be total storm in a teacup as far as I can see, and I imagine they'll end the evening in a four-poster bed together while I eat dinner alone."

"Sounds less than fun for you."

"Definitely. I can't leave just as my brother-in-law has come, but I'm extremely keen to escape the mad house and see you again. So, I know it's rather short notice, but would you like to do something tomorrow night?"

"Yes, I'd love to."

"I'd invite you here, but you can probably imagine why it's not the right time. Shall I book us a table again at that restaurant in your village, the food was very good last time."

"Actually." Morgana paused as an idea blossomed in

her head. "Would you mind if we went a bit downmarket? I'd like to go to The Fisherman's Rest, a pub in Lower Portmage. The food is terrible, mostly freezer stuff that's deep fried, and their wine list is pretty basic."

"Sounds delightful," Oliver said, laughter in his voice.

"I know, I'm not selling it. But I want to observe someone, part of a murder investigation."

"Another murder investigation? Are you helping the police again?" Oliver said.

"It feels more like they're helping me this time. Do you remember that ghost?"

"The one that may or may not have been a poltergeist?"

"Yes, which thankfully she's not."

"She?"

"Yes." Morgana smiled thinking about how powerful Valeria had turned out to be compared to a normal ghost if there was such a thing. "Anyway, I've been busy trying to solve her murder, and the police are now finally on board as we've found her body. But I'll tell you all about it when I see you."

"Sounds exciting, I look forward to it. Shall I pick you up? About 7.30?"

"Lovely, see you then, Oliver." Morgana felt immediately as light as air.

He *did* still want to pursue a relationship with her, despite how kooky she'd come across on their first date, and that boded very well.

Ten minutes later, her phone rang again. This time it was Tristan, and Morgana was very pleased with herself that her heart didn't race the way it had when she'd seen Oliver's name come up.

"Hi, I know you were planning to visit Rhiannon in hospital tomorrow, but they're releasing her. She's booked Taxi Tony to pick her up at twelve."

"Thanks, Tristan. I'll call Tony and cancel it, and collect her myself. It's much nicer having a friend get you and I don't think she knows many people in the area yet. That's great news she's well enough to go home."

She spent another few minutes on the phone after Tristan had hung up, calling first Tony and then arranging for her part-time worker to cover the shop for the following day.

Lancelot twined around her ankles as she went upstairs, being loving until she fed him, after which he totally ignored her.

"I know you're annoyed I was out all day, but I'm hunting a murderer, much like you hunt mice," she told him. "And unless the police can turn up something about Valeria's ex-boyfriend, then I think we're back to my theory that it's one of the women who liked Archie. But which one? We can rule out Bethany now, but that still leaves Belinda and Maud. Maud had financial motive as well, and seems more likely, but I'm not going to rule out Belinda either. Which reminds me, I must pay a call on Archie in the morning."

Lancelot proceeded to stick one leg in the air and lick his bottom, giving her a strong hint she was boring him, so she made dinner and had an early night with a book.

The following morning, she was up early to spend a couple of hours in the shop getting it ready for Lily.

Lily came promptly at ten as arranged. "I'm sorry about the short notice," Morgana said.

"No worries. I'll take all the extra hours I can get at the moment. My family is massive so Christmas always wipes me out financially. But at least I get a staff discount in here." Lily picked up a Yule candle and brought it with her to the desk. "Actually, this is perfect for my sister, though she'll probably expect me to spend a bit more."

"There's a nice, handcrafted candle holder made of beech that goes with it, if that helps?" Morgana pointed it out.

"Perfect. Though at this rate, I'll spend more than I earn being here." Lily pulled a funny face to show she was only joking, and Morgana felt very grateful she had such a cheerful second pair of hands. She'd have to up Lily's hours to make sure she didn't lose her to one of the other businesses looking for reliable staff.

"I'll be off then," Morgana said. "Are you sure you're okay to lock up later?"

"I could run this place for a week, no problems, if you ever wanted to take a holiday or anything?" Lily said.

"I'll give it some thought. I wouldn't say no to a break away from Portmage sometimes."

Morgana climbed into her old Land Rover and sat for a while, waiting for the engine to warm up. She loved the big beast, but it took a while to sound happy in the cold crisp air of winter.

"First stop, Crook Lane." She drove through the village to the far end and pulled up outside Archie Dawson's house.

He answered the door looking cheerful, but his face

hardened when he saw her. "More questions, Miss Emrys?"

"Who is it?" a voice called from inside.

"Morgana Emrys. The girl who was with the police," he called back.

"How wonderful! Tell her to come in, I want her to know our news."

Morgana barely recognised the voice, it sounded so happy. She was used to Mrs. Musgrove being quiet and sad.

Archie looked sceptical but gestured her to come inside and Morgana followed him into the kitchen.

"Oh, Morgana." Mrs. Musgrove jumped to her feet and surprised Morgana with a hug. Morgana wasn't big on hugging, but the aura of warmth and contentment radiating off Mrs. Musgrove was rather pleasant, so she allowed herself to be pulled in for a few moments.

"Morgana, Archie and I are getting married, and it's all thanks to you!"

Archie ran a hand through his hair, looking embarrassed. "I know it seems rather soon, after you only just found Valeria's body, but well... We've already wasted ten years."

"Don't be silly," Morgana said. "I'm very happy for you both, and wish you a much more peaceful marriage this time, Mrs. Musgrove."

"You have to call me Beth. I'd like us to be friends, and I'm not going to hide away anymore. I'm planning to go and see your mother later too, and some of my other old friends, and see if I can get a life going again."

Archie groaned. "I'll just stay here and do some weeding. I'm not sure I'm ready to face the world yet;

after all, most people still think I killed my wife."

"Actually, until the real killer is caught, it might be safer for you both to stay in for a while. I think it's someone targeting people you give those gold scarves to, though goodness knows why. Do you remember the first one you gave to Rhiannon was destroyed? And then she was attacked not long after you gave her another? The police are quite sure the same person who attacked her was the person who killed Valeria."

"Oh my." Bethany clutched at her chest. "Did she manage to say anything about who it was?"

"Unfortunately not, she was hit over the head first, same as Valeria. Also, let's not forget you were attacked too, Beth. Didn't you say the only thing they took was your scarf?"

"That's awful." Archie got to his feet. "I should get rid of the rest of them before I put anyone else at risk."

"Well, that's actually why I've come today, I was wondering if you'd let me have one. I might be able to use it to draw out the murderer."

"I don't think using yourself as bait is a very smart idea, Miss Emrys."

"No, I know it's not, but I won't be alone when I go out wearing it. I have a burly date for the evening and until then I don't think anyone is going to attack me in broad daylight out in public."

"They did with me; it was dark, but I was in a public place," Bethany said. "I just wish I'd seen who it was. They must be pretty clever, Morgana, to have attacked that many people and not been seen."

Morgana spread her hands. "It's the best idea I've got, and until the killer is caught, neither of you is going to be able to lead a normal life. Beth, you're at risk, and Archie, don't you want your name cleared?"

"Yes, but not at the price of anything happening to you."

"Just one evening, and I'll get it back to you tomorrow," she promised.

"No, you can keep it." Archie went to the box in the hall and withdrew a golden scarf. "But please, please be careful."

Morgana parked her car in Wadebridge Hospital Car Park and made sure her new scarf was plainly visible as she walked down the busy main street. Her next stop was the charity shop where Maud worked, which happened to be next door to a florist where she planned to get Rhiannon some flowers.

"Hello," she greeted Maud as she entered. But if she'd hoped for some reaction to the scarf she got none, just a sour-faced blank look.

She wandered around the store, hoping to find at least something she could buy which would give her a chance to interact with Maud. The shop was full of customers and Morgana reluctantly dampened down her witchy senses, trying to tune out all the frantic Christmas shoppers whose emotions were bombarding her.

She settled at last on a porcelain figurine of a child holding a stack of books, which she hoped Rhiannon could use as a shop decoration and took it to the serving counter.

"You were the one who found Valeria, weren't you?" Maud said, taking her time removing the price sticker. "I *told* you she was dead."

"Oh, you *do* remember me? I wasn't sure you did."

Maud gave a brief nod. "Saw you at the bookshop opening too."

"Really? Sorry, I didn't see you or I'd have come to say hello."

So, Maud *had* been at the bookshop on the night of the opening.

"Didn't go in. Too crowded."

Maud gave an irritated sniff and then began wrapping the figurine in tissue paper. "Saw Archie there too, bit morbid returning to the scene of his crime."

"Haven't you heard? The police cleared him; it seems he had an alibi for the time of her murder after all."

Maud's eyes rose to Morgana's face in surprise. "He did?"

"Yes."

Maud stared at the bundle of tissue paper, lost in thought.

Suddenly, her eyes filled with tears. Morgana held her breath, waiting to see if Maud would say something to incriminate herself. Instead, she went into a flurry of activity, ringing up the purchase and bundling the gift into a bag.

"I wanted to speak to him, but I saw that barmaid there too," she said, shoving the bag into Morgana's hands.

"Belinda?"

"No, the other one. Excuse me, I need to make a phone call, need to apologise." Maud spun on her heel and disappeared though a door marked Staff Only.

Morgana stared after her, completely confused. She

regretted she hadn't been able to focus her abilities enough to see Maud's aura, because she was quite sure it would have been very interesting.

"And just who the heck is the *other one*?" Morgana muttered as she left the shop and began to walk back towards the hospital, completely forgetting the flowers.

Chapter Nineteen

"How are you feeling?" Morgana asked as she drove herself and Rhiannon back to Portmage.

"Grateful to be alive, I suppose. Grateful to you too. Not only did you save my life but also, coming to pick me up today was so kind. I know you have a business to run."

"Hey, us small business owners need to stick together. Especially us single women business owners; it's no small thing."

"I feel the same," Rhiannon agreed. "Though I don't think it matters if you're single. I see so many women nowadays starting up as self-employed. Running a small business from their spare bedroom when the kids are at school. I bought these wonderful handmade earrings, and the cutest bookmarks from a tiny online store this mum of five had managed to create in her limited spare time. It makes me really proud to see those women juggling family and a business. It gave me the confidence to follow my own dream, even if it's over before it's begun."

"I have a lot of respect for those kinds of people too, but why do you say your dream is done?"

"Well, my bookshop is a crime scene now. Who knows when I'll be able to reopen? And someone doesn't want me around, plus I look a total state."

"All those things are only temporary. You'll be back on your feet in no time, the store will be a much better place for not having a body under it, and the murderer will be caught."

"Do you think so? They've got away with it for so

long, and I don't know that I feel safe in Portmage anymore."

"The police have more incentive to catch them now it's officially a murder, and so do I," she said, thinking of all the people who were at risk until it was done. "Whereabouts do you live?"

"Next left and then right, at 12, Freezing Lane."

"Really? You're right next door to Mrs. Musgrove."

"I've not had a chance to meet any of my neighbours; I've spent nearly all my time at the bookshop. It's a gorgeous little cottage though. I really thought I was living the dream moving here. My own bookshop and a little stone cottage. I'm only renting it and I'd planned to buy something in the village if the bookshop wasn't a total failure, though I doubt I'd ever get anything with the amazing sea view I have now."

"Funnily enough, I have a feeling the cottage next door might be coming up for sale soon." She couldn't imagine Bethany would want to stay in her house now she was marrying Archie. It clearly held a lot of bad memories for her.

"That would be wonderful. Assuming the murderer is caught, and I stay, that is."

"You will." Morgana was determined to make it happen.

After settling Rhiannon back in her home, Morgana went back to her own place to get ready for her evening with Oliver.

At exactly 7.30, just as the church clock chimed the half hour, Oliver knocked at the door.

"Very prompt," Morgana said, with a smile as she

opened it.

"Naval training. I can't seem to help myself. I'm thinking I probably need someone to come and shake up my well-ordered existence."

"Your sister?" she quipped.

"Ha ha, definitely not, they left his morning, thankfully. I was thinking of someone a bit more weird, someone who'll always say the unexpected."

"Ah, your grandmother then."

He didn't answer, instead pulling her in for a kiss.

When they finally broke apart, he said, "You. I want a bit more of you in my life. Now, get your coat or we'll be late. The reservation is for 7.45."

Morgana tutted at him. It wasn't even as though they needed to book at the Fisherman's Rest, as there would be plenty of free tables on a weeknight. But she got her coat and added the lurid gold scarf, making sure it was on top of her collar rather than under it. She might not have had much of a reaction from Maud, but she was hoping she'd get more of one from Belinda, or perhaps even this other barmaid Maud had mentioned.

Of course, Maud could just be very good at keeping a poker face with a bit of misdirection on the side.

They decided to walk down to Lower Portmage, taking the steps cut into the side of the cliff and then strolling across the beach to the pub on the far side. Morgana couldn't help watching Oliver as he went down in front of her and couldn't understand how he was still single at thirty-five. He was in excellent shape, broad-shouldered and weather-tanned from being outside a lot, and very calm and controlled. She felt relaxed in his company, almost peaceful, and suddenly, she could imagine lazy Sunday mornings, just being together, maybe doing the crossword, maybe taking a boat out on the sea. She felt no urge to fill the gaps in conversation. He didn't need it, and she liked that a lot.

The pub was busier than Morgana expected, probably down to having a roaring log fire on the cold winter's night, and several couples were eating.

Perhaps the food had improved since her last visit? She doubted it though, if the smell of chips coming from the kitchen was anything to go by.

"Let's get a drink from the bar first," Morgana said, guiding Oliver that way.

"Okay, but then you really do have to tell me what all this is about."

Morgana scanned the staff, looking for likely candidates. Belinda was there, pulling a pint of Guinness while laughing at something a customer was saying. Morgana couldn't open her senses in the bustling environment, but she didn't need them to see Belinda's laughter was strained and she was tired of being over-friendly. The other staff consisted of a much younger barmaid who was getting more attention and was moving around much faster fulfilling orders, and a fifty-something man she recognised as the landlord, who was a raging alcoholic and clearly only pouring drinks for himself.

Morgana flicked her scarf as she finally got Belinda's attention. "What would you like?" she asked Oliver.

"Just a half of bitter for me."

"A half of bitter and a gin and tonic please."

"No problem, love." Belinda began to pull the half.

"Busy in here tonight," Morgana commented,

fiddling with the scarf again, letting the light catch on the glittery bits.

Belinda nodded, her eyes on the scarf.

"It's nice, isn't it. Didn't you used to have one similar?" Morgana knew she should play it cool, but it wasn't really in her nature.

"That's right. I liked it, I did, but it wasn't made to last. Fell apart after a year or so. Amazing you even remember."

Was that a hint of suspicion in Belinda's voice? Morgana couldn't be sure.

"Five pound fifty please." Belinda put the drinks down in front of Morgana. Oliver made a move to pay but Morgana was faster. "My turn, remember?"

Oliver made a huffing noise but let her do it. "Now I know why you wanted to come here instead, it's considerably cheaper than the last place." He gave her a wink to show he didn't mean a word of it and Morgana elbowed him in the ribs.

"Next time, I'll cook for you," she said, her voice laden with promise, and Oliver gave her a narrow-eyed glance.

"*Can* you cook?"

"All witches can cook; it comes with the territory. Hubble bubble and all that."

"Lovely. Eye of newt, my favourite. Shall we find our table?"

Once they were seated and had given their order to the waitress, Morgana began in a low voice to tell him everything that had happened over the last few days.

"So, you actually think our barmaid," his eyes flicked to the bar, "could be the murderer? She looks like somebody's grandmother. Not my grandmother, who would rather die than wear leopard print, but somebody's grandma."

"They were all ten years younger when it happened, and anyway, older people want to find love as much as young people."

"My grandmother would tell you you're crazy, and the best years of her life were after her husband had the sense to cock up his toes."

"Your grandmother is about ninety, rich, and a few apples short of a barrel," Morgana retorted.

"Can't argue with that." He held up his hands in mock surrender. "But still, she looks as though she'd rather have a warm cup of cocoa and curl up with a cat than go and murder someone over a man."

"Well, it may not be her. I wonder if there are any other barmaids working here? The other one who's on tonight is definitely too young to be a suspect."

"A lot of women go for an older man; you can't rule someone out for being younger than Mr. Dawson."

"No, that's true, but I can in this case." Morgana tilted her head at the other barmaid as she went past. "She's not even twenty. She'd have only been nine or ten when Valeria was murdered. It was past her bedtime."

"You have a very interesting hobby, Morgana. I just hope it doesn't put you in any danger."

"You're not the first person to say something like that today," Morgana said, finally shrugging out of the cloying scarf. "To be honest, I'm not sure if my efforts have been even remotely worth it this time. I haven't managed to get rid of the ghost and I'm no closer to finding out who did it than the police were ten years ago."

"You've cleared an innocent man's name, that has to count for something. And Valeria's body has been found so at least the police can now treat this as a murder and not a missing person."

"I guess. So, tell me some personal things about you, I feel you're a book I haven't read yet and I only know the back cover copy."

Oliver smiled. "Isn't that the best of a relationship? The learning. I think we're all looking for someone we can spend years and years getting to know and they'll still surprise us with something new even after all that time. I only wish I'd be a more interesting read, like you are."

"You're interesting to me because you're so very *different* to me. You're a peer of the realm, you grew up in a mansion, and yet your grandmother told me you used to sleep in a tree house and keep a pet mouse in your pocket."

"Little boys are the same the world over; they want adventure, but need security." His eyes turned serious. "There are a few wild years in my past after my parents died, but then I had to grow up and come home, otherwise we'd have lost the house and the land, and with it the title. But a mansion isn't a home unless it has a family in it."

Oliver covered her hand with his and Morgana suddenly felt rushed. Through the physical contact between them, Morgana instantly got flashes of insight into his mind.

He spent months at a time stuck out into the middle of nowhere, with little chance to meet someone to share his life with. He'd felt immediate chemistry with her and its intensity had surprised him. It had also horrified him a little, but he was determined to discover if it was meant to lead somewhere.

Morgana pulled her hand away before she saw any more. She'd only ever had one long term relationship and it had ended very badly. She valued her independence and wasn't sure she was looking for anything serious. Oliver clearly was.

"Talking of family, tell me about Mozart; has she had her kittens?" Morgana changed the subject. When she'd spent the weekend at Oliver's mansion, he'd been feeding a stray cat. A cat who was always enticed inside to listen to him play the piano, so he'd named her Mozart. Morgana had been the one to break it to him that Mozart wasn't a boy, but instead a very pregnant female.

"She has, right in the music room as you predicted. I bought her a posh bed, and bowls, but she chose an old cardboard box instead, and still prefers stealing scraps from the kitchen despite me putting out real cat food. We have five kittens, a complete mixture of colours, so goodness knows what their father looked like. You should come and visit them, they're real characters."

"I'd like that."

They spent the next ten minutes exchanging cat stories until their food arrived and then set about eating. The quality of the meals had definitely improved since Morgana's last visit, and though it was still very much pub fare, at least the ingredients seemed a bit fresher. Conversation moved on to food and then films and books, the very standard sort of getting-to-know-you topics.

When the meal was over, the tide had come in, so crossing the beach was impossible and the bottom of the steps they'd used to come down were now under water. So they walked back up the hill, taking the road to Portmage village.

"Did you get the reaction you were looking for, with the scarf?" Oliver asked.

"Not really, but I couldn't use my senses to see her aura, not with so many other people around. If I open them up then I get everything, all the pain and greed and negativity around me. It's not pleasant."

"I thought everyone looked like they were having a good time tonight?" he said, confused.

"They were, but the other stuff stays, swirling under the surface of the happiest-looking people. It's amazing how much sadness there is behind a lot of smiles, and I have to feel it all whenever I try to read anyone in public."

It was at that moment Morgana became aware of the car.

The night was dark now and cars normally slowed right down the moment their headlights picked out walkers on the road, but this car didn't. In fact, it sped up.

She had a moment to sense the fury and then she gathered all her energy.

Oliver realised the danger a second later and tried to reach for her to pull her to safety, but he was too late. She took the energy and blasted him as hard as she could, sending his body crashing into the hedge beside the road.

As the car ploughed into her, Morgana felt as if time

slowed down.

She felt her knees buckle and then she catapulted over the bonnet. For a long moment, she made eye contact with the driver and then hit the road again—and everything went black.

Chapter Twenty

Consciousness came with a painful jerk. Everything hurt. She couldn't move yet or open her eyes, but her brain was already putting everything in place. The other barmaid. Not from the Fisherman's Rest, but from the Knights at Arms, ten years ago. Barely more than a teenager, collecting glasses. She could hear Oliver's voice in her mind saying, "Sometimes, younger women go for older men." And she'd been there at the bookshop opening, she'd tried to talk to Archie, she'd worn the golden scarf.

"Morgana?"

Her eyelids flickered as she realised Tristan was beside her, holding her hand.

"It was Jennifer, Jennifer Penwyn," she said, her voice coming out very croaky.

"We know. Just relax. Can you manage a sip of water?"

She opened her eyes to see him lift a glass, fastening her dry lips around the straw sticking out of it.

"Not too fast."

"How bad is it?" she said, when she'd had some water.

"Pretty bad. Now isn't the time for me to tell you how stupid you were, but if Lord Latheborne hadn't been there, you'd have died. You were bleeding out from a severed femoral artery. But he used his shirt to stem the bleeding and make a tourniquet. Very professionally done and it saved your life. Definitely the kind of man you want around in a crisis."

"How did you know it was Jennifer?"

"Lord Latheborne was also quick-witted enough to memorise the number plate. After he phoned an ambulance, he called the station and we picked her up half an hour later. She was completely raving. Insane probably."

"How long have I been out?" She tried to sit up but Tristan pushed her back down.

"Nearly twenty-four hours. You went into surgery late last night and you're in a recovery room now; you're going to be okay, but pretty bruised for a while.

"It's just amazing you didn't break both your legs. It looks as if you took the immediate hit on the back of your knees, which was the best scenario, but I'm afraid you lost all the skin down your back when you hit the tarmac. It'll probably leave some scars, and so will the operation on your thigh."

"Where is Oliver? Is he okay?"

"He hasn't left the hospital since you were brought in; he's pacing around the waiting room, along with your mother and your sister, who are doing their nut because I haven't let anyone in here. In fact, you've had a whole host of visitors. Rhiannon stopped by with a pile of books, and Mr. Dawson and Mrs. Musgrove brought flowers and a veg box.

"Your shop assistant said she has the store under control and you mustn't worry about that, and Ellie said to tell you she's fed your cat. So, you have nothing to worry about. Do you feel up to seeing anyone? I'm not sure I can keep your mother out of here much longer."

Morgana nodded, then groaned with the pain of movement. "I'll see Mum and Ellie first, then Oliver if he doesn't mind waiting?"

After her mother and her sister had fussed over her for a while, they eventually went, and Oliver came into the room. He looked very tired and was wearing a sweater that clearly belonged to someone else. She remembered Tristan saying Oliver had used his shirt to bandage her up, but she supposed his jumper had probably been covered in blood too.

Her blood.

He took her hand a placed a kiss on the back of it. "How are you feeling?"

"Sore, but grateful to you," she answered.

Oliver shook his head.

"You have nothing to be grateful for. You took the brunt of it when it should have been both of us. You…" He paused and swallowed. "You got me out of the way, yet we weren't touching."

Morgana gave him a look of almost pity. This was the crunch point.

"I used magic."

"Magic? You threw me several feet with magic?" He still sounded sceptical.

"Yes. That's really the only physical ability I have at the moment, and the adrenalin gave it most of its power, but that's the truth." She waited to see how he'd take it.

Oliver ran a hand through his hair. "Okay."

"Okay?"

"Yes. I nearly lost you and I'm not ready to do that. I'm still in if you are."

She nodded and he bent to kiss her forehead. "You look exhausted, I'll leave you to rest now. But how about a weekend break at Latheborne Manor? I've just hired a new housekeeper and between us, we can wait on you hand and foot?"

"I'll think about it," she promised, her eyes already closing again.

Ten days later, Morgana hobbled into Lebeau Books on crutches.

Most of her bruises had gone down and her back was healing nicely thanks to a special poultice from her own homemade creams and lotions sold in her shop, but her leg was going to take a little longer.

"Morgana." Rhiannon rushed over to help her onto a sofa.

"Hi. It's my first day up and about, so I thought I'd come here and return the books you lent me."

"Don't be silly, you could have kept them."

"Yes, but then I couldn't swap them for even more."

"How are you feeling?"

"Good. Everyone's been very nice, especially Oliver."

She blushed slightly, thinking of the long weekend she'd spent recuperating at his mansion. Not that she'd been strong enough to do much unless you counted solving another mystery while she'd been there. But the coiling tension between them was extremely satisfying in its own way, and she enjoyed the anticipation of knowing there was more to come. Playing with all the kittens had been good therapy too.

"I'm glad you're here. I wanted to ask you about Valeria. Nothing has happened since I've come back to work and I wondered why."

"That's actually the other reason I came." Morgana took a long look around the shop, before softly calling out, "Valeria?"

She waited, but there was no answer. "She's gone. It happens that way. When her killer was caught, she was set free."

"Oh." Rhiannon looked sad. "I would have liked the chance to say goodbye."

"Me too. But it's better for her."

Morgana felt just as low as Rhiannon about Valeria disappearing without anyone to see her on her way, but she also knew the dead didn't feel regrets once they'd moved on.

Valeria would be at peace now.

"Well, I'm going to keep the haunted theme going in her memory. Maybe a trick shelf or something that pushes out an occasional book."

"Good idea," Morgana approved. "People around here like that kind of thing."

"I still can't believe it was that young woman; she seemed so normal. I hear she was ranting about Valeria making Archie's life a misery and him being trapped in a loveless marriage. She thought she was setting him free and it was only a matter of time before he returned her feelings, so long as no one else got in the way first. Total madness, especially as he was hardly aware she existed."

"Maybe that was part of the madness? If she obsessed from afar, then she could keep the illusion going in her mind, but if she actually got close to him, it might have revealed the truth of his feelings. Tristan told me her psych evaluation revealed she had all kinds of issues.

"She lost her mother when she was born and then her father left her with an ancient relative while he went off and had a series of girlfriends. I guess she just bottled up a lot of anger towards the women she felt replaced her with her father, as well as seeking out a new father figure in Archie Dawson? That's what the police psychiatrist suggested anyway." Morgana shrugged. "But none of that excuses murder. It seems she was working at the Knights at Arms the night Valeria was killed, which is only just up the road from here. She must have slipped out right after they called time on the bar, so no one noticed."

"Well, we're all a lot safer with her locked away. It's crazy she targeted anyone who was given a scarf. I've stopped wearing all mine now."

Rhiannon touched her bare neck and gave a shudder.

"That's the scary thing about crazy," Morgana said. "You never know who's hiding what beneath the surface."

But as she accepted a cup of tea and looked at Rhiannon's warm and caring aura, Morgana realised there *was* someone who sometimes knew. *She* did. She had the power to see it, and despite the many lectures she'd had recently on being more careful, she knew she'd continue to use that ability to help the police wherever possible.

"Now, let's see," Rhiannon said, stacking up the books Morgana had brought back. "What would you like next? Some more romance novels?"

"Do you know, I think I'm about ready for a juicy murder mystery, maybe with a Christmas theme. Just for a change, you know?"

They both laughed, and a sea breeze went through

the shop, closing the door once and for all on the mystery of the ghost in the bookshop.

Stella Berry

Books in this series

Murder Most Pumpkin (prequel)
Body at the Bakery
Killer at the Castle
Murder at the Mansion

www.stellaberrybooks.com

Would you like to know what Morgana did while she was staying with Oliver?

I'm currently writing **The Mystery of the Latheborne Diamonds**, which will be released exclusively to my Reader Group in September 2021. Join the group on my website, and get your *free copy* of **Murder Most Pumpkin** at the same time!

www.stellaberrybooks.com

Recipe: Stinging Nettles as a side dish

Like any witch, Morgana likes to cook with plants that grow in the hedgerows of England. And stinging nettles are a regular witch's favourite.

A lot of people are put off using them because, of course, stinging nettles sting! However, once cooked, the sting is gone, and they are both delicious and nutritious.

Cut the nettles by the stem, and make sure they are under two foot otherwise they tend to get a little tough when taller than that (I definitely advise wearing gardening gloves to hold them). You can eat the stems, but I don't recommend it as they are a bit less tender. Instead, carefully snip all the leaves away from the stem and into a bowl and rinse them thoroughly (as you should with anything picked in the wild).

Next warm some butter or good olive oil in a frying pan and add the nettles. Keep stirring so they don't burn for about four minutes until they are all soft, then season with salt and pepper.

Serve as a tasty side dish with any meal. That really is it, so get out there and cut some nettles!

Printed in Great Britain
by Amazon

78462978R00107